Sweet Wicked of Mine

Paranormal in Manhattan Mystery: Book 5

By Lotta Smith

Copyright

Sweet Wicked of Mine© 2017 Lotta Smith.

Cover copyright 2017 Viola Estrella

Editing and proofreading: Hot Tree Editing

All rights reserved.

No part of this book may be reproduced or transmitted in any form or by any means, electronic or mechanical, or by any information storage and retrieval system, without express written permission from the author/and publisher.

This book is a work of fiction. The names, characters, incidents and places are the products of the author's imagination, and are used fictitiously. None of the characters in this book is based on an actual person. Any resemblance to locales, actual events, or persons, living or dead, is entirely coincidental and an unintentional.

The author acknowledges the trademarked status and trademark owners of various products referenced in this work of fiction, which have been used without permission. The publication/use of these trademarks is not authorized, associated with, or sponsored by the trademark owners.

To hear about new books and

discounted book sales, please sign up for my newsletter at:
   http://eepurl.com/bOSLYj
   And follow me on **Amazon:** http://amzn.to/22h0TSf

PROLOGUE: Jackie

Detective Jamie Alabaster read the case file over and over, feeling edgy.

She was investigating a serial assault/murder case happening near Pier 26, and Jackson Frederick Orchard, a Broadway actor, was the latest victim.

Though she was desperate to find the killer of the three innocent people and one other severely injured person, she was running out of time. Not that she was terminally ill or too old to expect tomorrow to come like any other day, but she was leaving the NYPD in a few weeks. Her family ran a high-end sports bar and restaurant near Yankee Stadium for generations, and her father decided to retire early. As an only child, she didn't have much choice not to succeed him at the establishment, and obviously, a detective's salary was just a fraction of the earnings coming from the family business.

Reading through the case file for the umpteenth time, she finally realized what had been bugging her. She'd met all the family, friends, and acquaintances of the latest victim, but one of them triggered Jamie's sixth—or seventh—sense as a detective. On the surface, the person—a choreographer from the *Aladdin* production, which Jackson had been working on just before his untimely death—seemed like a quiet, soft-spoken guy, but she felt an eeriness about him. She couldn't exactly pinpoint the cause, but she sensed a sinister vibe.

As she rallied her courage to pay him another visit, her desk phone rang.

"Hello?" she answered.

Words escaped her as the caller informed her Ryan Francine, the man who Jamie was going to meet, had died in a car wreck just a few hours before.

* * *

Almost five years later...

The sky was blue with just a few small clouds floating like little piles of cotton candy. The wind was quiet, and the Hudson River was calm. Reflecting the rays of sunshine, the river almost looked like a mirror. A couple of young, attractive, openly gay males kayaked down the river, breaking the tranquility, turning the mirrorlike surface of the water into an actively flowing stream.

On the greenway by the river, people jogged, worked out, and walked the dogs. Everyone was smiling, laughing, high-fiving with their loved ones—looking happy and carefree.

Jackson Frederick Orchard, a.k.a. Jackie, sat alone at a table in the outside garden of City Vineyard at Pier 26.

Watching the happy people coming and going across the riverside walkway for fun and exercise had been *her* favorite pastime when *she* used to be a budding actor.

Jackie liked to be addressed as a female, and she was blessed to have friends who treated her as a lady without questions or argument. There were times when she was a male actor who was often described as a heartthrob among female audiences, but nowadays, gender didn't mean anything to Jackie anymore. After all, touching someone was physically impossible—much less hugging, kissing, or making love.

When an elderly couple, probably in their seventies, was escorted to her table, Jackie waved at them. "Hi, there! How are you? It's a beautiful day, isn't it?" But neither of them acknowledged her, nor smiled. Jackie wasn't saddened or offended by their response.

She was used to such reactions—or lack thereof—from most people, and she understood their reaction wasn't based on discrimination against her. For the majority of people, someone like Jackie was simply imperceptible—because, after all, she was dead and her body didn't exist in this world anymore.

Sometimes, she appreciated their inability to recognize her. No thanks to getting killed on the night of Pride Dance, she had been stuck in a skintight, neon pink tank top and a skimpy, neon green skirt. Her hair was big and messy, sporting a white boa headdress, and her heels were sky-high. Her necklace screamed 'FESTIVE,' which was inappropriate on occasions, like a funeral. Not to mention the huge knife sticking out of her side and a portion of her gut peeking out of the wound weren't flattering her looks.

The couple at her table ordered a glass of wine each before looking at the lunch menu.

Sitting at the same table as them, Jackie

learned that the wife's name was Mandy and the husband's was Rick. Jackie's eyes widened in amusement. She knew a young couple with the same names. Mandy happened to be one of very few people in this world who could communicate with Jackie. Rick couldn't see or hear dead people, but he was a topnotch FBI agent, and with Mandy's help, he'd been trying to find the person who killed Jackie.

Almost five years back, Jackie was stabbed to death, and the killer hadn't been caught. Following the first three and a half years, she was practically nonexistent, for no one could see or hear her. When she found Mandy—or rather, Mandy found her—Jackie's dead life had changed. To be exact, it was as if she'd gotten another life to live.

She knew her friends were working hard to find her killer between the many cases they handled. As the saying goes, a crime scene is like Treasure Island in terms of information. Jackie often returned to the place she was killed in hopes of finding information about her killer. But at the same time, she was becoming less and less optimistic about her killer being identified, much less caught. The case was cold, and the detective who'd worked it had retired.

Jackie stared at the greenway where she had been walking at the time of her death.

On that night, she was excited. As a proud member of the LGBT community, participating in the dance party was not only fun but inspirational. Even after five years, she could still visualize the fireworks at the end of the party when she closed her eyes. She'd become acquainted with new people on the dance floor at the pier. One of the boys was devastatingly cute, and she'd felt huge potential for a romance with him. Aside from that, what truly made her happy was her blossoming career. After the years of lessons, followed by minor roles and working as one of many backup dancers, Jackie had finally nailed a larger role on Broadway.

She had been walking along the greenway with her friends, but at some point, she found herself stranded in the party crowd. When a man passed by her side, she considered him to be one of the partygoers, but then he turned back and approached her. He was clad in a hooded black costume, and his face was invisible. At first, she thought the man found someone he knew behind her, but he came toward her.

A dull pain throbbed in the side of her abdomen, and Jackie knew something wasn't right. She reached down and discovered warm, wet liquid. To her horror, a large knife was sticking out of her painful belly. She opened her mouth to scream for help, but her voice failed to come out.

Meanwhile, her attacker stood there, twisting the blade deeper into Jackie, not uttering a word.

Recalling the night she died, Jackie couldn't help but wonder if she would have made it to stardom if she were still alive. In the week following Pride Dance, Jackson Frederick Orchard was supposed to stand on the stage of the New Amsterdam Theater.

She took a deep breath and shook her head in an attempt to forget about the future she might or might not have had. As they say, there's no point crying over spilled milk. Thinking about the future she could never have was a waste of time.

The couple at her table was discussing whether to order desserts as appetizers. Listening to them, Jackie wondered if the Mandy and Rick she'd known for over a year would end up like this mature couple.

CHAPTER 1

Excited about seeing the New York City Ballet's special gala, she walked down the promenade at David H. Koch Theater in Lincoln Center, shooting selfies with her phone—she was totally active on Instagram—and enjoying every step of her way back to her seat located at orchestra level. The uncharacteristically warm and sunny Saturday in March made her yearn to stroll through the sand in Long Beach, but she had no complaints. The loveliest part about visiting Long Beach was driving there from Manhattan, but she didn't get to drive anyway. She loved ballet, and having no school for the day helped lift her mood.

Her name was Julie Grey, a third grader at a certain private school in the Upper East Side and a future prima donna at some elite ballet company such as the New York City Ballet, or a supermodel, or an A-list actress and a great philanthropist—at least, those were her aspirations.

For the time being, she was walking on her own like an independent woman, and she absolutely loved it. Actually, she went to the powder room with her mom, Meredith Grey—she wasn't making her mom's name up. It was her real name, which hadn't been an issue until the TV show popped up—who met an acquaintance there. In Julie's opinion, her mom could talk practically forever when she was on a roll, and Julie often wondered how her mom handled her job as a doctor who had to see many patients every day. Anyway, Julie decided to sneak out, and there she was. Sometimes, a girl needed her privacy.

It also made her deliriously happy and excited that she caught a glimpse of Rick Rowling at one of the boxed suites on the balcony. He was tall, muscular, and had the most beautiful face. He was one of her parents' long-time friends, and Julie had known him for her entire life of eight years. Rick was more gorgeous than any stars on the big screen, but what made him more adorable was that he happened to be an FBI special agent who caught bad guys. How cool was that? Also, he was the heir to a huge security-based company called USCAB and had been once selected as Mr. Number Two of the most eligible bachelors in New York City. In Julie's opinion, the judges had poor tastes in men, because Rick should have been voted Mr. Number One.

At school, girls often gossiped that Tom Thiel, one of the heirs of a financial giant, was really cute—not to mention obscenely rich—but she knew Tom was merely a little kid who happened to be born with a silver spoon. Besides, the name Tom Thiel had way too much resemblance to Tom Thumb for her preference.

Rick was different from any popular boys at her school. Not only was he totally, devastatingly hot and sexy—yes, being young didn't mean she couldn't understand the exact meaning of "adult" words, did it?—but he called her by her favorite nickname, Jules, and he treated her like a human with her own personality, not a big baby who occasionally had temper tantrums. Whenever she was around Rick, and especially when he looked at her with the most intense green eyes, she felt her heart pitter-pattering. She was so in love with him!

Julie was happily toying with the idea of visiting him in the boxed suite—she could even talk her parents into letting her join Rick during the performance, so they could have a nice chat—but then she spotted a woman walking in front of her, chattering and giggling, even though she was alone.

Julie wrinkled her nose. She had seen that woman called Mandy not just once but three times. Each time should have been a happy moment for Julie because she'd unexpectedly bumped into Rick, but Mandy was tagging along with him like toilet paper hanging out of his pants. Julie didn't like that. Okay, so Rick was a playboy and Julie was used to seeing him with a lady friend, but she rarely saw him with the same girl more than once. If she recalled it right, Mandy was partly responsible for Rick's injury the previous summer. Julie couldn't figure out why he'd bothered to accompany Mandy so often.

Unlike other women Julie had spotted with him so far, Mandy was neither a supermodel, A-list actress, nor a socialite. She was merely his assistant. On top of it all, Mandy was a total weirdo who spoke to herself way too much and way too often. She was totally unsuitable for Rick. Julie knew he deserved better—no, he deserved the best—someone with beauty, sophistication, and grace. She wished Mandy wasn't his date for the ballet gala.

Watching Mandy talking and laughing to the thin air, Julie grew curious. *Who's she talking to? Does she seriously believe she has an invisible friend only she can communicate with? If so, she's truly crazy.*

Mandy didn't seem to notice Julie, her romantic rival—yes, she should take Julie as serious competition—watching, so Julie decided to ambush her in hopes of uncovering Mandy's dirty little secret. Stan Goldman, one of Julie's classmates, was always saying something about the best defense being a good offense.

"Mandy, what's so funny about this pillar?" Julie asked, sneaking up from behind.

"What? Oh!" Gasping and jumping about a foot, Mandy displayed a forced smile at Julie. "Wow, it's you, Jules. Hi! How are you?"

Julie looked back at Mandy disapprovingly. She hated how Mandy called her by her special nickname. Anyway, she said, "Hello, Mandy. By the way, who were you talking to? And I prefer to be called Julie. You know, Jules is reserved for my closest friends."

"Oh, well... okay, Julie." Mandy glanced to the side, looking a little taken aback, but she recovered soon and went on. "I was on the phone, you know, using a hands-free device."

"Really? If so, why don't I see an earbud in either of your ears?" Julie pointed out. She didn't miss that something was forced in Mandy's tone. She was hiding something from Julie. Why else would she gasp and jump like that if she had no secret? The place was a public corridor after all, and anyone could talk to her.

"Um...." Mandy felt for her ear with no device, but after a pause, she hurriedly changed the subject. "So, Julie, I heard you've been practicing ballet very hard. Are you here with your mommy?" She spoke to Julie like a pediatrician talking to a preschool patient.

"Oh yes. She met someone at the powder room, and I guess she's still chatting." Julie shrugged, and then she gave Mandy a head-to-toe once-over. She knew it wasn't nice, but she couldn't help it. Unlike Rick's other dates, Mandy was on the chubby side. "I didn't know you're interested in ballet. You've never practiced ballet, have you?"

"Actually, I took ballet lessons in my youth, like a couple of times," Mandy said, "but I wasn't on friendly terms with gravity, and I'm not that crazy about ballet. Dan was the one with tickets, since he was invited, but he decided to skip the event, saying he's seen more than his life's share of ballet, so he gave them to us."

"Excuse me? Did you just say *us*?" Julie inadvertently demanded in a very unladylike manner, but again, she couldn't help it. After all, Mandy called Rick's dad by his first name! Julie had known Rick far longer than Mandy did, but she still called his father Mr. Rowling. Apparently, Mandy was acting too familiar with Rick's family. How dare she!

"Yes, I did?" It sounded more like a question than a statement, Mandy tilting her head to the side.

"I thought you were here on your own," Julie

said, trying her best to sound nonchalant and hoping Mandy was just bluffing about coming with someone else when she was really solo.

"Actually, I came here with Rick." Mandy butchered Julie's hopes with one sentence. Also, something like a happy glow appeared around Mandy when she said his name.

"Oh really?" Julie said casually, trying to conceal her shock. "I thought he was with Bella, one of his many girlfriends. She's a dancer, socialite, and a model. She's soooo pretty. You know, Rick's a known playboy who changes his date more often than he replaces his socks." She used a staged whisper, thinking that little piece of information was likely to rattle Mandy.

"Wow, I didn't know he changed his dates that often. As far as I know, he seems to change his socks at least once a day." Mandy chuckled lightheartedly. It wasn't the reaction Julie was expecting. She didn't seem to be shocked.

"Julie, you know a lot about Rick, don't you?"

"Of course." Julie lifted her chin. "I've known him since I was a baby. He's my first-ever BFF." As she said that, Mandy's attention turned to the empty space beside her. Eyes widening, Mandy gasped like she saw something shocking. Julie took it as a delayed reaction to her previous comments about Rick's wild dating habits, so she went for another strike. "You know what? He's got soft spots for delicate, beautiful girls like models. Perhaps that has something to do with him having a ton of art expertise and—" Julie was going to imply how Mandy wasn't

Rick's type, just to make her point, but her little speech was interrupted in midsentence.

"Well, well, well, you must be Amanda Meyer, the person who solved the McCambridge case."

Julie looked back and her jaw dropped. Behind them stood Maleficent.

Okay, so, Snow White was a fictional character and so was her villain mother, but the woman looked as scary as the fairy-tale villain, or perhaps scarier. She was clad in a black lacy dress and black stilettos with red soles. Sporting lots of huge diamonds on her fingers and neck, the fairy-tale villain was carrying a small jeweled purse. Julie recognized Maleficent from somewhere, but she couldn't come up with the name.

Julie glanced at Mandy, who was opening and closing her mouth like a goldfish. She looked truly uncomfortable—much more so compared to when Julie had previously made not-so-nice remarks. She didn't turn her head, but her eyes flickered around like she wanted to run away from Maleficent.

"Is that you, Ms. Westwood?" Mandy mumbled, as if she were unsure, and Julie finally recognized Maleficent as Aurora Westwood, the celebrity psychic who had her own TV shows.

"I heard so much about you from Miranda. When I heard about how efficiently you handled and closed the case, I was impressed." Aurora came closer to Mandy, who raised her left hand as if she were trying to protect herself.

The moment Julie spotted a beautiful ring of

pink stones forming a four-leaf clover on Mandy's ring finger, she found herself thinking about the worst-case scenario—the ring being a gift from Rick. Julie shook her head in an attempt to convince herself that she was being paranoid. Still, she could tell the ring wasn't something a mere assistant could afford. Julie closed her eyes, silently begging God to please let it be a false alarm.

While she tormented herself with the grim prospects, Aurora stared into Mandy's eyes with the same passion she displayed on *Breaking Dawn with Aurora Westwood*, one of her TV shows, in which she helped the troubled visitors using her power as a prophet and psychic medium. *"I'm looking at everything you're trying to hide!"* was the key phrase the psychic used on that show. "How interesting! Look at your aura, it comes in so many unique colors."

"What do my aura colors tell you about me?" Mandy asked, averting her eyes from the scary psychic.

"So many things, including something words cannot fully describe." Aurora's blood-red lips formed a wide grin, and then she suddenly turned to Julie. "Hello, sweetie. What's your name?"

"I'm Julie. Julie Grey."

"Oh, hello, Julie. By the way, you have a very beautiful aura." Before Julie had a chance to turn away, the psychic caught the girl's eyes. "I can see you're so pure, innocent...."

A part of Julie wanted to run away because the old woman in front of her had some mystic air, and Julie was afraid to have her jealousy over Mandy pointed out. As she looked into Aurora's icy blue eyes, shivers crawled down her spine, and then she felt numb… until a deep, strong voice boomed in her ears.

"Well, well, well, if it isn't you, Aurora." A large man in a glossy black Italian suit and a top hat in matching fabric walked toward them.

"It's you, Brian. What a nice surprise to bump into you!" Aurora switched her gaze from Julie to Brian Powers, a budding exorcist. "I didn't know you're a ballet aficionado." She raised the corners of her red lips into a courteous smile, but her eyes weren't smiling.

Julie scurried to his side. She was familiar with Brian Powers, who covered her from Aurora's view by protectively standing in front of her. Brian was another friend of her parents.

"Actually, I happen to greatly enjoy the ballet," Brian said lightheartedly, displaying his own courteous smile, but just like Aurora, his eyes weren't smiling. "I suppose someone within the company needs your spiritual guidance, am I correct?"

"Oh no. No one in our business talks about the clients. Besides, I'm here solely for pleasure, so let's not talk about work."

"Really? Then why do I see your assistant when it has nothing to do with your work?" Brian raised one of his eyebrows, looking at a middle-aged woman accompanying the psychic like a lady-in-waiting.

"Because it's Ms. Seymour here, my

secretary, who is a true ballet connoisseur." Indicating the woman with one hand, Aurora said, "Sometimes, you have to entertain your help." Following Aurora's words, the woman's mouth twitched. Julie saw two moles lined up on one corner of her lips. For some unknown reason, Julie thought they looked like eyes—not smiling eyes but sad ones trying their best to keep from wailing.

  The woman called Ms. Seymour was like the shadow of her employer. Clad in a drab black suit without makeup or accessory, she looked pale, rail thin, and ghostly.

  "Excuse me, but have we met before?" Mandy abruptly asked the secretary.

  "I'm afraid not," Ms. Seymour replied in a small voice, not meeting Mandy's eyes.

  "So, Mandy, since when have you been friends with the most celebrated psychic?" Brian glared at Mandy.

  "Oh no, it's my first time meeting her, you know."

  "I had heard so much about your friend with the FBI, so I couldn't help talking to her the moment I spotted her," Aurora said breezily.

  "Hmm, so what's your take on her?" Brian asked, frowning.

  "She's incredible. She has an aura coming in colors I've never seen. I'm utterly impressed." Aurora gave Mandy a sideways glance, prompting her to shiver.

  "Excuse me, Ms. Westwood, but the show will begin shortly," Ms. Seymour whispered to

Aurora in a hesitant tone.

"Oh, what a shame. We've got to go." Aurora shrugged and took a small black card out of her jeweled purse. "Amanda, you have to come to my place so we can have a nice chat over tea."

"Um… well…." While Mandy babbled in apparent panic, Aurora forced the card into her hand, turned on her heels, and started walking toward the theater.

Brian crossed his arms as he watched the TV psychic and her secretary walking away. When the two women were out of earshot, he muttered, "I don't like this. Did you see the way that monstrous woman looked at you? It was as if she was putting a curse on you. You've got to be careful. That bitch is famous for her evilness."

"Will you stop using bad words, Brian?" Mandy shushed him, stuffing the card in her purse. "We have young ears with us."

"Are you talking about me?" Julie chimed in, coming out of her hiding place behind Brian. "For your information, the B-word is not enough to shock me. I'm not that naïve. Fred Michaelson at school is even bragging about knowing the meaning of the F-bomb."

"Oh really?" Brian flashed an amused smile. "That's interesting."

"Julie Harper Grey! Don't even think about telling what you were thinking about telling. You've already shared too much information with my friends," Meredith Grey, Julie's mother, scolded her daughter as she trotted toward Julie in her Manolos.

"By the way, sneaking out of the powder room and leaving your mommy behind wasn't nice, young lady."

"Sometimes, a woman's got to have alone time," Julie protested, pouting. "And I didn't wanna miss the beginning of the show. We're here to watch the gala, not to spend two hours at the powder room listening to the conversation between you and an acquaintance of yours, remember?"

"Of course, I remember." Meredith winked and turned to Brian and Mandy. "Thanks, guys, for babysitting my little princess."

"Meredith, you might seriously want to watch her back. Aurora Westwood was looking at Jules like some high-end dessert," Brian warned.

"Are you talking about the TV psychic?" Meredith perked up. "Seriously? Did I just miss her? I wish I'd have gotten here sooner."

"No! You're lucky to miss her." Mandy did a full-body shiver. "She was so scary."

"Right. That witch is evil," Brian agreed.

"If only I could unsee her!" When Mandy swiped her left hand from side to side, like she was trying to erase the memory of her encounter with the psychic, Meredith took her hand.

"Hey, look at your ring. It's an antique Bvlgari, isn't it?" she exclaimed, looking at the beautiful pink stones forming a four-leaf clover. "This is sooo beautiful. I love it!"

"Thanks."

Mandy blushed, prompting Meredith to gasp and say, "Oh my God, it's from Rick, isn't it?"

Julie willed Mandy to say no. At the same time, she promised God that she'd consider eating Brussels sprouts if only he'd have Mandy deny her mom's question, but obviously, God wasn't listening to Julie's request.

"Yes. It was Christmas gift from him. Talk about a surprise gift!"

Meredith shrieked, high-fiving with Brian, who apparently tried to keep a straight face and failed to do so.

Julie was beyond devastated. For a split second, she contemplated breaking down, curling up in the corner, and crying like a baby. But instead, she raised her chin and stomped her little feet, declaring, "I will never, ever eat Brussels sprouts! I'm not going to even touch that evil vegetable!" just to make her point to the heavens—and to keep her dignity, of course.

"You have a point, Jules. Brussels sprouts are evil," Brian agreed, gently patting his little friend on the head.

Meredith looked at her daughter, raising an eyebrow. "Fine, but then you're better off eating kale anyway."

"That's not the point!" Shrieking, Julie clung to Brian. She knew he wasn't much of a hugger, but she was in desperate need for someone to cuddle.

CHAPTER 2

On Tuesday afternoon, I was at my desk in the office located in the furthest corner from the one occupied by the head of the FBI's New York City field office.

It was a slow day with no new cases, and Rick Rowling, my boss and only colleague in the Paranormal Cases Division, was participating in one of those mandatory physical training sessions. I was on my own in the office, killing time. While I was adding some finishing touches to the latest case report, the ring on my left hand jumped into my sight, prompting me to smile like a total idiot. I knew it was lame, but I couldn't help it.

"Hey, girlfriend, what's up?" Jackie popped up from out of nowhere and got in my face, hanging upside down like a pet parakeet who got bored with its regular position.

"Yow!" I shrieked in half surprise and half horror.

"Come on, Mandy, will you stop reacting like you've just seen a ghost?" She pouted.

I took a deep breath, then said, "Okay, here's the thing. First of all, I'd appreciate it very much if you'd give me some warning, or a knock at least, before sneaking up on me à la Spider Man, or some creepy villain in a horror flick with your otherwise beautiful hair totally covering your face. And secondly, you *are* a ghost."

Yes, you heard me right. Jackie, the drag queen, clad in a revealing outfit in neon colors, happened to be a ghost, and I wasn't hallucinating.

I'm Amanda Meyer, but most people call me Mandy. I used to be a medical student, but following wicked twists of fate, I landed a job working as a special assistant to Rick Rowling at the FBI's Paranormal Cases Division. I happen to communicate with dead people, and in my opinion, my reaction to being ambushed by Jackie was totally justifiable. Considering she'd appointed herself as my guardian angel, the ghost had a tendency to spook me.

"You know what?" Jackie continued nonchalantly. "According to Carina Christien, trying on new things sprinkled with the element of surprise is what makes your life exciting," she said, mentioning a certain bestselling author Rick and I had previously encountered, then flipped herself up into the normal position like an astronaut repositioning herself in weightlessness and grinning triumphantly. As she did, the shiny, long blonde hair bounced back onto her shoulders and her necklace screaming 'FESTIVE' gleamed.

I did a mental forehead slap. "What? Have you been sneaking up on my Kindle device?"

"I need entertainment when you're not available," Jackie said matter-of-factly.

"Brian said you're always welcome."

"Oh yes, except he's a little scary. Can you believe he made me learn his aura by heart on Saturday? If I describe yours as soft, fluffy, and somewhat sweet, his aura is sharp, hard, and well…

spicy! Yeah, spicy is the word. Anyway, he makes me feel uneasy."

"You know what, Jackie? You're sounding like you have a crush on Brian," I teased, prompting the ghost to do a full-body shiver.

"By the way, you have to set your screen timeout at the max," Jackie went on. "It's totally frustrating when the screen dies on me when I'm in the middle of reading. Oh, don't forget to turn on automatic page-turner. Hey, don't look at me like a stalker. I need entertainment while you and Rick are in the bedroom. You'd hate it if I interrupted you in the middle of a hot, steamy, X-rated—"

"Ooookay, so you can read anything you'd like using my Kindle!" I snapped before the flamboyant ghost went into too much detail.

"Ooh, Mandy, you're sooo cute when you blush like that." Jackie chuckled lightheartedly, moving her hand as if she were patting my shoulder. "By the way, I totally love the four-leaf clover. I'd be grinning nonstop if I had such a beautiful ring on my ring finger. It's totally swoon-worthy. Not to mention it's from Rick." She whistled.

"Thanks," I said, trying to keep a straight face, only to fail. As I touched the ring I couldn't help grinning. Not only did I absolutely love this Christmas gift from Rick, but it was something that signified the blossoming relationship between the two of us.

When I met him for the first time, I was detained at Chapel Hill Police Department, being falsely accused of a triple murder—for some unknown reason, three people who'd previously committed violent crimes, but slipped out of the justice system unpunished, dropped dead just minutes after touching me—and Rick came in and cleared my name. Under normal circumstances, I would have fallen in love with him. After all, the devilishly hot and devastatingly sexy FBI agent had practically saved my behind. Except, while proving my innocence, he also gave me the unpleasant nickname of "Grim Reaper," resulting in my expulsion from medical school. So, when I started working with the FBI as his assistant, I couldn't have been more unenthusiastic.

At that time, he was my least favorite person, and I couldn't even imagine befriending him, much less dating and living with him. But following a freak accident in which he broke an ankle, we'd been living together and now he introduced me as his girlfriend. The ring he gave me was tailored to fit the fourth digit of my left hand and… okay, sometimes I spent hours trying to decipher the meaning of his action without success. I knew that the easiest and perhaps the most dependable method of disentangling the mystery of the ring size was to simply ask him, but a part of me was too scared to do so because his answer may not be something I'd want to hear. Anyway, the old saying about life being full of surprises was so true.

Jackie started to giggle abruptly.

"What's that supposed to mean?" I asked.

"Hey, Mandy. I think I've just developed a skill to give you a prediction. Wanna hear?" she said, still giggling.

"What prediction?"

"Be solemn and listen carefully, for I'm telling this only once."

"Jackie, why are you sounding like a fortune teller in Coney Island?" I chuckled, but the ghost of a drag queen kept a straight face and made tsk-tsk sounds.

"Listen carefully." She stuck out her index finger. "I have a hunch that the love of your life will pop *the* question pretty soon."

"*The* question? What's *the* question?" I said nonchalantly, but of course, I knew what she meant.

"Are you playing dumb or what?" She snorted, pointing at my ring. "Seriously, he gave you this. No guy gives you this unless he has serious thoughts about you including marriage, and I'm positive Rick's totally serious about you."

"You think so?" I whispered, even though we were alone in the office.

"I am," she replied, also in *sotto voce*. "Remember when Dan visited you guys for dinner a few weeks ago? When you went to the kitchen to fetch dessert and wine, Dan suggested to Rick that it's about time to leave the feds and join the family business, and Rick didn't reject that proposition."

I opened my mouth, then shut it. I knew Rick was going to leave the FBI someday, as he'd take over USCAB—United States Cover All Bases—as the sole heir to the multibillion-dollar conglomerate, but I didn't see that coming so soon. Dan was full of energy, looking like he'd be capable of running the conglomerate for the next quarter century. Of course, even Dan can't live forever and Rick would have to take the place of his father. But I wasn't expecting that day to come so soon.

"But the juiciest part is this: Dan told him to settle down with a family, and Rick replied, 'Yeah, it's about time,' which led to my prediction."

My jaw dropped. "Okay, let's take a deep breath." I took a deep breath, and then another. So, Jackie's story definitely had potential for the big M-word, but I didn't want to hold high hopes until I heard the exact words from Rick. As the optimistic side of me demanded thinking about the future and dancing happily, the pessimistic side shrieked that I stop holding on to groundless hopes. I felt light-headed.

"Anyway, I suggest you try not to fill in the companionable silence with unromantic topics such as this guy who tried to rob a fish and chips shop with a banana. I know he loves your funny traits but sometimes humor can kill romance." Jackie went on, and she gasped. "Mandy, are you hyperventilating? Okay, calm down. Put your hankie over your mouth and nose and hold your breath."

I did what I was told and I felt better.

"Feel better?" Jackie furrowed her eyebrows.

"Yes, I'm feeling better. Thanks," I said, still gasping.

"Okay, sorry about rattling you." Jackie moved her hand as if she was attempting to clear away my panicky reaction. "Let's talk about something more laid-back, shall we?" and I couldn't agree more.

While Jackie and I chatted about Tom Ellis, the ghost's latest fave actor, the door to the office opened and Rick came in.

"Hey." He waved at me.

"Hey." I waved back, my heart fluttering at the sight of him. "How did the training session go?"

"Same old, nothing special. Running, jumping, target shooting, sparring, and sweating like a horde of pigs. This so-called training makes me appreciate my weekly training at the MMA gym. Then again, sometimes I feel like such a dope for training for training sessions." He shrugged, standing at 6'2" with a body that practically looked like a model from Calvin Klein men's underwear collection, he was looking sharp, clean, and deceptively refreshed for someone who'd just participated in vigorous exercise. Not even a lock of his hair set in a conservatively messy 'do was out of place. He sat at his desk in the deepest corner of the office. "By the way, Mandy, we don't have any fundraisers or galas this week, do we?"

"Let me see." I took out a small journal sporting Gudetama, the lazy egg, from my purse. "You're right. We have nothing scheduled this week."

"Don't forget we have to watch *NCIS* tonight," Jackie chimed in. "The previous episode was a cliffy, and I absolutely have to watch tonight's episode. So, I'd recommend you eat at home."

"Oh, I got that." I nodded at Jackie, prompting Rick to ask, "What?"

"Jackie says we have to watch *NCIS* tonight, and she doesn't want us to eat out."

"Okay, in that case, we can order something. What would you like? Pizza? Chinese? Deli from Dean and Deluca, or…?"

"Hmm… deli sounds nice." As I closed the journal, something fell on my desk. It was a black card with letters sprinkled in gold. "Oh, yikes!" I muttered.

"What's that?" Rick looked at the card.

"It's the card Aurora Westwood forced into my hand at the ballet theater on Saturday."

"The TV psychic?" Rick raised one eyebrow. "Why did she do that to you?"

"She said Miranda Wolff, whom we met on the Giselle McCambridge case, told her about me. I don't know… but she's creepy."

"I know!" Jackie jumped in. "Creepy was an understatement! One moment I was having fun watching you get interrogated by Julie, and the next thing I knew, that witchy woman appeared and I couldn't breathe. I thought I was going to be killed."

"Could it be possible for you to die twice?" I asked Jackie, and then I conveyed her words to Rick.

"Jules interrogated you? That must have been quite a sight." Rick chuckled. "She can be pretty fierce."

"Yeah, I think she'll make a great detective," I admitted, recalling the encounter with her. "She spotted me chatting with Jackie, and she kept on asking me who I was talking to. I said I was using a hands-free phone, but she didn't buy that."

"What a shame that cutesy girl couldn't see me." Jackie shook her head. "It would have been nice talking to a little girl for a change."

I resisted the urge to roll my eyes. Considering her nosiness, Julie would have asked Jackie a ton of questions if she could actually see the ghost of a drag queen. I closed my eyes and then opened them again, hoping the card would disappear like smoke, but it was still on my desk. "It's so creepy. I threw it into the trash box on my way back to the seat, but now it's back with me like a cursed object," I said, picking the card up with the tips of my fingernails like a piece of dirty laundry. "On top of all that, she told me to visit her."

Rick whistled. "Sounds like an irresistible invitation. When are we going?"

"We? I'm not going anywhere near her, thank you very much." My fingers trembled as I said it.

"Mandy's right, Rick. She was sooo scary!" Jackie emphasized.

"By the way," I said, remembering the woman tagging along with the famed psychic, "Aurora's secretary was with her. I recognize her from somewhere, but I can't recall where I met her. And it's been bugging me."

"Do you know her name?" Rick tilted his head to the side.

"She was called Ms. Seymour, and that's all I know. I should have asked her for a card."

Then Rick's cell phone chirped. "Hello? Hey, Meredith, what's up? How's Jules? ... What the hell?" The conversation started breezily on his side, but the lightheartedness disappeared immediately. His face suddenly turned expressionless, his jaw visibly tense. "Where are you? Did you talk to Ben? Have you contacted the local police? What about USCAB? Okay, they'll start working with the FBI's Child Abduction taskforce. Stay put. I'll be there in fifteen." Then he disconnected the call.

"Was it Dr. Grey? What's happened?" I asked.

He took a deep breath. "Jules is missing. She always carries her GPS phone, but it's been disabled and her whereabouts are unknown."

I gasped. "That doesn't sound good."

"I know." Rick frowned. Then he looked around midair, saying, "Jackie, perhaps watching *NCIS* tonight has to wait."

CHAPTER 3

"Meredith, let me take a look at the latest photo of Jules," Rick told Dr. Meredith Grey, his long-time friend from kindergarten, as soon as she let us into the penthouse on the Upper East Side.

"Her photo? Digital or paper?" she asked in a quivering voice. I met her for the first time last summer when Rick hurt his leg, and I still remembered how she treated him efficiently, with occasional wise-cracking. My impression of her was like an orthopedic surgeon version of Wonder Woman, who always looked perfect while sporting sassy attitude. But this time, her normally perfect complexion was blotchy and her pixie hair looked more disheveled than fashionably messy. Her shock and panic were palpable.

"Paper would be better, but digital can do," Rick said, crossing his long legs while sitting on the cushy sofa in the Greys' living room.

We weren't the only visitors at the Greys' residence. Two men in dark suits were working with laptop computers. According to Rick, they were tactical security consultants from USCAB, the security-based conglomerate run by Rick's father. The USCAB agents had already set up devices so they'd be able to trace calls in case the Greys received a ransom demand.

"Okay." She didn't look convinced but stood up from the sofa and scurried to the mantelpiece decorated by family photos. "How about this one?" She brought a framed one.

"Mind if I remove the frame?" Rick asked.

"No, go ahead." When she handed the photo to him, her hands were visibly trembling. "Rick, Mandy, I'm so glad you guys are here with me. I know I can't blame my husband for performing emergency surgery, but for a moment, I truly, desperately wish I married a pathologist... or even an unemployed guy instead of a neurosurgeon." She hugged herself. "Am I babbling?"

I made sympathetic sounds. "No, I get your point perfectly. Pathologists tend to have more work flexibility as they deal with dead patients most of the time." The moment I said it, I wished I could rewind the time.

"Dead...? Oh my God, now I know why Rick asked me for Jules's photo. You know if a person is dead or alive just by looking at the photo! I thought you've been joking, but you're serious, right? What if my baby's...?" She started wailing and I moved by her side, patting her arms. "The police are doing a door-to-door search, and this specialist lady from the FBI dropped by, but...."

Rick raised an eyebrow, but he only said, "Okay," as he removed the photo from the frame. In the picture, Julie was triumphantly smiling in a ballet tutu. He stared it for a moment, then said, "She's alive, and she's not in any immediate danger."

Meredith took a deep breath. "Are you sure? On a scale of one to ten, where ten means 'Hell yes!' how much do you rate your sureness?"

"I'm positive that Jules is alive, and as for the score, I'd say ten out of ten," Rick assured her. "So far, I've never been wrong about my prediction."

Meredith bit her lower lip as if to fight the urge to break into a full-blown sob. Taking a deep breath, she said, "Fine. I believe you. At least, I can try."

According to her, Julie usually went to her grandparents' home located just two blocks from the Greys' condo. As it was Tuesday, the governess, who was also a French tutor, was supposed to accompany her from the school to Meredith's parents' home. The school administrator witnessed Julie leaving school with Bell Sandburg, a master's student at Columbia. Under normal circumstances, they should have arrived at the grandparents' home in less than thirty minutes, where they would converse in French for another hour.

An hour after they had left the school, Bella called Meredith in a panic, saying she'd lost Julie on the way. According to Meredith, Bella recalled strolling the sidewalk with Julie, heading for Julie's grandparents' condo. She remembered feeling slightly dizzy at some point, and the next thing she knew, she found herself standing in front of Bloomingdale's on Lexington. To Bella's shock, she was all alone and Julie was nowhere to be seen. Bella had no memory of how she'd migrated from East 79th to Midtown. She was uninjured and didn't recall being abducted or assaulted, but she couldn't remember when and where she parted with her student.

Following the phone call from Bella, Meredith

immediately left work early and contacted the police, USCAB—which was the Greys' security company—and Rick. Bella was being held in custody at the NYPD as a person of interest.

"How about ransom demands? Did you get any?" Rick asked.

"No." Meredith shook her head. "The police seem to be regarding Bella as a suspect, but… I don't know. To be honest, I can't imagine Bella taking my daughter away. She's from a very good family, and she got along well with Julie. As for mental status, I've never sensed anything unstable or odd about her." She took a deep breath. "Besides that, Bella's story about zoning out, wandering off in the middle of streets, finding that she'd lost Julie—that sounds too doped and confused, doesn't it? People sometimes do the stupidest things, but Bella isn't one of them. If she'd come up with a scheme to stage Julie's kidnapping, she should have a better excuse than the one she's provided."

"I get your point." Rick nodded. "Suppose Bella was responsible for Jules's disappearance. She would have vanished without calling you, and you'd already have received ransom demands. I agree that 'I have no memory about it' sounds too lame for an excuse."

"Dr. Grey, Mr. Rowling." One of the USCAB consultants approached us. "We have located the area where the signal from Julie's phone was last detected."

"Good, Dalton." Rick nodded. "By checking the security camera feeds in the neighborhood, we should be able to find out what happened when Jules's phone was switched off."

Dalton furrowed his eyebrows. "It's strange. The security camera seems to have been disabled at the time of Julie's disappearance."

"What?" Rick frowned.

"No apparent glitch in the network has been reported, but footage in this particular area turned out to be dark nothing. The tech department's working to identify what caused this issue, so…." Dalton fumbled with his words, looking uncomfortable.

"Where's this area? I mean, where was Julie's phone last detected?" I interjected before Rick opened his mouth. "The security camera might have been disabled, but we can talk to witnesses." After all, it wasn't like Julie disappeared in the middle of nowhere.

Dalton looked at Rick, who said, "Go ahead."

The location happened to be just three blocks from the Greys' condo. Rick thanked Dalton and turned to Meredith. "Take a deep breath and stay home, okay? We'll visit the area to obtain any information about Jules."

"But…." Meredith frowned, looking unconvinced.

"Trust me," Rick said, patting my shoulder. "Mandy here has a knack for bumping into witnesses even the most skilled investigator misses."

"Please save my daughter," Meredith whispered as we left the Greys' condo.

* * *

The signal from Julie's phone was last detected in the promenade between Madison and Park Avenues.

"Right. Any info about this matter is highly appreciated. My line is open twenty-four seven. Okay. Talk to you later."

While Rick was on the phone a few yards away from me, I squinted, furiously looking for ghosts. My plan was to find one who might have witnessed Julie just moments before her disappearance. That was something I'd prided as my kind of work. Generally speaking, ghosts tended to find me and talk to me at the worst possible times—such as when the food had just arrived at the restaurant, or the moments when Rick was about to kiss me—but this time, I literally couldn't find a soul of a dead person.

It was getting dark, and I bit my lip in worry. "Is anyone here?" I called to the blank space in hopes of contacting someone, but no matter how hard I tried to find ghosts, I couldn't see any. Frustrated and panicked, my heart started pounding. My cheeks were burning, and I was about to start hyperventilating.

Then I heard footsteps and Rick held me from behind. "Mandy, relax." He pulled me close to him.

"I can't," I mumbled. "How can I face Meredith if we don't find Julie safe?"

"Forget it. You won't do a better job by freaking out," he whispered into my ear. "Pretend it's one of our regular cases about total strangers. It's not easy, but stop taking it personally. Now, take a deep breath—in and out."

I closed my eyes and did what I was told.

"It's not like finding a needle in a haystack. Ghosts usually find you when you least expect it." Muttering softly, he stroked my hair with his nimble fingers.

"Rick...." I leaned my head on his chest. His big strong hand was still caressing me, and I felt so safe. Though it wasn't the best or appropriate moment, I was secretly expecting—or rather, wanting—him to kiss me... until someone cleared their throat.

I opened my eyes, gasping, "Oh, Jackie... it's you!"

"Jackie, found any witnesses?" Rick said to the air, releasing me from his embrace. He couldn't see or communicate with the ghost of a drag queen, but he knew Jackie could hear him.

"Oh, don't bother with me," Jackie teased, making a kissy face. "I can wait till you two finish making out."

"Um...." I cleared my throat. "So, any news?"

"Okay, guess what? I just found a guy stuck nearby. He might have seen Julie," she said, pointing across the street in front of us. "Look, there's a brownstone building across the street behind the streetlamps, the one right next to the white building with a macaroon shop downstairs. I think he's stuck in there. I tried talking to him, but he hasn't responded to me. Perhaps you can grab his attention."

I looked carefully at the place Jackie had indicated. "Over there? I think I see a blurry, whitish shadowlike thing by the building."

"That's him." Jackie nodded. "Wanna go say hi?"

"Of course." Then I turned to Rick, pointing at the direction of the brownstone. "Jackie found a ghost who seems to be stuck in this neighborhood."

"Good. Let's go." He took my hand and we started walking.

We crossed the street and approached the brownstone. As I came near the building, I started to see the blurry silhouette of a teenage boy standing with his shoulders slumped.

I pointed at the ghost several feet away. "He's over there."

"Uh-huh. Talk to him."

"Sure." I nodded and approached the ghost. "Hello?" When I spoke, he didn't seem to notice me.

He stood there unmoving, as if he'd been turned into stone. His head was bent down toward his Gucci loafers. Though rumpled, he was clad in designer clothes from head to toe. His shirt caught my eyes. It was so avant-garde with one pale blue side and crimson on the other.

"Hi there! I like your shirt. It's from Brooks Brothers, isn't it?" Jackie attempted to strike a conversation while floating in the air.

The boy didn't seem to notice her, so Jackie raised her voice, bouncing around him. "Hello? Can you hear me? I hope you can hear me 'cause there's something I want to ask you!"

As Jackie went on with her quest to get the boy's attention, he slowly raised his head, looking sleepy. "Um… you are…?" Looking at the ghost of a drag queen, he tilted his head to the side. As he did, I noticed that it was his blood staining his shirt crimson. Assuming from the huge gash on his head, the cause of his death looked like a fall from a high place. I resisted the urge to flinch as I looked at the boy ghost and imagined the impact he'd had prior to his death.

"I'm Jackie. Meet my friends, Mandy and Rick." As Jackie introduced us, the teenage ghost's eyes widened.

"Can they see me?"

"Mandy here can see us, but unfortunately, Rick can't. What a shame," Jackie said breezily.

"Hi, I'm Mandy. Nice meeting you," I said, looking him directly in the eyes, prompting him to suck in air.

"Seriously? How many fingers do you see?" The teenage ghost made a V-sign.

"I see two fingers," I said. "By the way, we're looking for a girl named Julie. Did you see this girl at around two in the afternoon?" I showed him a photo of Julie.

"Was she wearing a pink down coat?"

"Yes." I nodded. "And a pair of black trousers. She was also sporting a navy Prada backpack."

"Oh, that girl." He cocked his head to the side.

"You saw her?" My eyes widened.

"Did he see Jules?" Rick nudged me by the elbow, and I nodded.

Looking at the photo, the ghost said, "I think it was this girl. The girl was strolling down the street with a young woman, and then the girl hopped in a black Mercedes and left."

"Oh gosh... she's been kidnapped." Jackie gasped.

"What happened to the young woman with Julie? Was she taken with the girl?" I asked. Assuming from Meredith's words, I thought it was highly unlikely that Bella let Julie leave like that.

"The woman who looked like a college student? As the girl—Julie?—hopped in the car, the older woman suddenly turned on her heels and left."

"Oh my God...," Jackie and I said in unison.

Rick frowned. "It's not good news, is it?" I shook my head and conveyed the information to him, and he groaned.

"Can you tell them more about what you saw?" Rick asked the blank space where the ghost stood. He couldn't see or communicate with dead people, but I was used to being the interpreter to convey dead people's words to him.

"Okay, can you see that low-rise condo over there? The white building with a red façade?" The teenage ghost pointed at a building located several yards away. "Julie was walking with the woman, and then the Mercedes drove by, slowing down before stopping by her side. I saw a middle-aged dude wearing a black suit driving the car. Then the window in the back seat rolled down and an old lady with heavy makeup talked to the girl."

"Did you catch the old lady's words?" Rick asked.

"I heard words like 'mom' and 'sick.' And I

think the old lady said 'hospital.' Anyway, the girl voluntarily hopped in the car."

"Hell," Rick groaned as I whispered the ghost's words to him.

"In retrospect, I sensed something fishy about the situation." The ghost shrugged his slender shoulders. "Then again, I couldn't do anything 'cause I'm stuck here."

"Can you describe the old lady's attire?" Jackie chimed in, sounding like a detective.

"I saw her black jacket. I didn't see much of her face, but I remember her thick makeup… especially the blood-red lips." The teenage ghost tilted his head to the side.

"Do you remember the car's license plate?" Rick pressed on.

"Well… no. I wasn't paying much attention." The ghost shook his head.

I relayed his words to Rick, who insisted, "Try harder. Can you at least remember some of the letters or numbers?"

The ghost furrowed his eyebrows. "Sorry, I really can't remember what was written on the plate. Besides, the distance between the car and me wasn't nice."

"I see," I muttered. The ghost had a point, but Rick didn't look pleased.

Crossing his arms, Rick said, "Fine. Don't hesitate to be in touch with Mandy here in case you recall more about the girl's abduction." Then he took a few steps to the side and pulled out his phone.

"To be in touch? Seriously?" The teenage

ghost displayed a cocky smile. "For your information, I can't make phone calls."

"Oh, right. You can't move from here." I nodded, exchanging a glance with Jackie. I was glad Rick was on the phone and I didn't need to translate the ghost's smartass remark to him. Rick himself had a habit of being a smartass, yet he detested when he was on the receiving end of such comments.

"I'll come and check on you regularly," Jackie volunteered.

"Thanks, Jackie, and…." I turned to the teenage ghost and stumbled with my words. "Gosh, I didn't ask your name."

"I'm Tyler McGraw," he muttered and closed his eyes, as if our brief conversation had exhausted him.

CHAPTER 4

After parting with the ghost of Tyler McGraw, we hurried back to the Greys' condo. The sky had fallen dark and lights from streetlamps and shop ads illuminated the neighborhood. The promenade was neither crowded nor deserted. I found it odd that the FBI and police struggled to find living human witnesses.

"Hey, Mandy, did you feel the ghost was telling the truth?" Rick asked me, putting his phone into his coat pocket.

"Well, I don't think he was actively lying, but…." I fumbled with my words.

"But what?" he pressed on.

"Something about him is bugging me, like he seemed to remember so much in detail," I said.

"Of course, he should remember things in detail. He witnessed the kidnapping of a little girl. In my opinion, his statement lacks info, like the car's license plate." He shrugged.

"That's because you're an FBI agent and Tyler's just a kid. He looked like a high school student," I pointed out.

"Besides, the boy was sleeping when we spoke to him. And it took him a while to catch our voice," Jackie chimed in. "I have a hunch he's one of those ghosts who sleeps through their post-life existence in this world. I was surprised he admitted to witnessing Julie's abduction. I was wondering how he'd managed to stay awake at the time."

"Hmm… perhaps he's most active in the afternoon?" I said, but it sounded more like a question than a statement.

"By the way, how did that ghost end up being bound to that place?" Rick said as I relayed Jackie's words to him.

"I thought about asking him, but I wasn't sure if it was appropriate to ask such a personal question on the initial encounter." I sighed. "So, Rick, how are we going to deliver the news to Meredith?"

"We'll tell her about Jules's abduction. The kidnapper might be someone Meredith knows." Rick shrugged.

"I know, but we can't possibly tell her about the source of information—like, 'By the way, we heard about Julie's abduction from a ghost of a teenager bound to that place'—can we?" As I looked up at him, he touched my eyebrows. "What are you doing?"

"Just smoothing your forehead," he said nonchalantly. "You don't want to have frown lines engraved on your face at this age. Oh, and don't forget that hassling yourself doesn't help with the case."

"Um… thanks?" I said, resisting the urge to frown and feeling really hot in the cheeks.

"Anytime." The corner of his lips quirked up into an angelic smile. "Don't worry about the informant. I'll do the talking, and you don't have to tell Meredith about your skill. Are we good?" he asked, taking my hand.

"Good." I nodded, tightening my grip on his hand.

I was worried sick about Julie. Being kidnapped was beyond horrible, and I felt even more horrible about delivering the grim news to her mom.

"Don't worry, honey. I'm always here to help you guys," Jackie cooed.

* * *

When we returned to the Greys' condo, Rick relayed the news about Julie's abduction and the description of the culprit to Julie's parents.

"Oh my God... it's like a nightmare. No, I hope it's a nightmare. At least with nightmares, the reality might not be that bad when you wake up," Meredith muttered as if she were having difficulty processing the news.

"An old lady in black, chauffeured around in a black Mercedes with a man in black? No, I can't say we have such an acquaintance." Ben, Julie's father and a hotshot neurosurgeon, furrowed his eyebrows as he squeezed his wife's hand.

"We've told Julie never to hop into a stranger's car." Meredith shook her head. "Especially considering Bella was with her. She adores Bella, and I can't imagine Julie ditching her and going for a joyride with an old woman she's not even familiar with."

"But isn't it odd? Why did Bella let the old woman take our daughter away? Doing nothing?" Ben frowned.

"That's a good point. It's odd." Rick crossed his arms.

"By the way, considering the captor was an old lady, the odds of her being a pedophile is very small, right? In that case, the motive for Julie's kidnapping should be money. If so, what's the kidnapper doing? She should be demanding ransom by now," Ben said breathlessly, and then he blanched. "Oh crap, the woman was old. What if she's after Julie's organs?"

"Stop it already!" Meredith snapped, clutching her hands into fists. "Don't even imagine that! We have to find Julie. Rick says she's alive and not in any immediate danger." Her voice was strong, but her knuckles were white and trembling.

"Oh… I'm sorry…," Ben mumbled, clutching his head with both hands.

An awkward silence filled the air, but when I glanced at Meredith, my eyes widened.

Jackie, who popped up from out of nowhere, was floating around the agitated mom, whispering, "Relax. Everything's gonna be all right. Now take a deep breath in… and out.…"

I resisted the urge to roll my eyes when the ghost of a drag queen winked at me as our eyes met.

Meredith didn't seem to notice Jackie's presence, but she appeared to have calmed down. "Gosh, I'm famished. I don't know what I want to eat, but I've got to eat something for dinner," she said.

Ben raised his eyebrows, looking like he was seriously considering rolling his eyes, but at the same time, he was smart enough to refrain from doing so.

"That's a good idea," Rick interjected. "This place will be packed with feds in no time, so it's clever to eat something while you can."

"If you don't mind, I'm more than happy to help you in the kitchen, Meredith," I volunteered, prompting Meredith to smile for the first time that day.

"Actually, I was thinking about ordering in, but yeah, it's better to have something to work on. Thanks, Mandy. I'd appreciate your help so much," she said, then led me to the kitchen.

The Greys' kitchen, smaller than the one at Rick's place, was full of topnotch equipment but managed to appear cozy.

"By the way, Rick said he found a witness at a brownstone building on East 78th. Was it the one right next to a white building with a macaroon shop downstairs?" Meredith asked while stuffing a head of cabbage into the chopper.

"Right. That's the one." I nodded, dumping canned tomatoes, ketchup, black pepper, and sugar into the sautéed mixture of ground turkey and chopped celery. We agreed to go with a simple dinner of turkey sloppy Joes and a side of coleslaw. "The neighborhood was populated, but it wasn't easy finding a witness."

"Oh no, not that building," Meredith muttered.

"What's wrong?" I asked, startled, wondering if I said something I shouldn't have.

"Oh, it's not your fault, but this boy named Tyler McGraw was found dead in front of that building about a year ago." She frowned. "I know a friend of his mom, and according to her, he was rumored to have committed suicide. The worst part was no one around him, including his parents, could see any reason for that."

I gasped, and so did Jackie. The possibility of Tyler becoming a ghost after committing suicide had crossed my mind, but I didn't have the heart to ask him for the cause of his death.

After a while, I said, "Look, Meredith," though I wasn't sure what I was going to tell her. "Julie is fine. I've known Rick for a while, and when he says Julie is fine, she's fine. You can trust him."

"I know I can trust him." She gave her a courageous grin. "Speaking of him, let's serve dinner to the boys. They must be famished."

CHAPTER 5

The following morning, Rick, Brian, and I were gathered at the dining room of Rick's condo on Fifth Avenue, having a meeting over breakfast. I adored Rick's lavish condo with state-of-the-art chef's kitchen and everything, but sometimes I missed the noisy, crowded living arrangement at my parents' home in Queens. At least I could always expect food to be served without my cooking.

"Why didn't you throw out that haunted card?" Brian Powers, one of very few exorcists who could actually cast out evil spirits, glared at me. "I told you that old bat is bad news. Evil is an understatement for Aurora fucking Westwood. If I may say, you shouldn't have accepted it in the first place."

I bit my lower lip, looking begrudgingly at the black card on the dining table. "I get your point, but you can't possibly say, 'Thanks for offering your card, but I refuse to have it because you scare the bejesus out of me,' can you? And in fact, I did throw it away as soon as I got away from Aurora. Okay, so I didn't and couldn't hurl it away in the middle of the theater's corridor like a total litterbug, especially in front of Julie, but I remember tossing it into the trash. After that, I'd totally forgotten about it but somehow it came back to me. I don't know how that card came out of the trash and jumped into my scheduler, and actually, I don't want to know how that happened."

"What? The card came back to you? Like one of those haunted antique jewelries? The worst part of this is that I can't tell you to shut up and stop lying to me." Brian took a gulp of coffee. "Where's your ghost pal?"

"Jackie? She went to have a chat with a ghost who witnessed Julie being taken away in a black Mercedes," I said. "Ghosts tend to be more open to fellow ghosts than they are to humans."

Brian snorted and turned to Rick, who was savoring the bacon and eggs on his plate. "So, what do you want me to do? I'm not that naïve to assume I was invited to breakfast just out of courtesy."

"Hey, Brian, ever heard of small talk?" Rick raised an eyebrow at Brian, who responded with an annoyed glare. Rick shrugged. "It's about Aurora Westwood. I need your insight about that TV psychic."

"What insight? Like that old bat is a monster?" Brian grimaced.

"Actually, Mandy suspects Aurora has something to do with Jules's disappearance. The amber alert has been issued, and Child Abduction Response Deployment and the NYPD are already working with their conventional ways. So, we're taking the unbeaten path," Rick said nonchalantly, touching my arm. "Also, I have a hunch that she's probably right."

"What? Are you serious?" Brian's eyebrows jumped up. "Okay, so that old witch has no such thing as standards. Also, the part about Jules's governess strengthens the theory that someone used some crooked magic. Her story about losing Jules on the way while she zoned out sounds too lame for an excuse, so perhaps it's not an excuse."

"Right. The cops and the feds regard Bella as the prime suspect. They don't believe her. Still, it's possible to mess with Bella's head and take away Jules in front of her." Rick looked at me. "Mandy, tell him about your experience during the encounter with Aurora at the theater."

I told Brian about the intense gaze Aurora had directed at Julie and how the psychic had complimented Julie's beautiful aura. "Also, there's this ghost of a young boy who saw an old woman with heavy makeup, dressed in black. According to him, this woman took Julie away. I know there are way too many old women in the city, but on top of it all, Aurora's ardent eyes directed at Julie has been bugging me ever since. You know, she creeped me out."

"I know. That witch is beyond creepy." Brian grimaced. "Hell, I should have warned Jules about Aurora the Evil."

"What's bugging me is I have no idea about Aurora's purpose in taking Jules," Rick muttered.

"Mandy." Brian frowned. "Aurora described Jules's aura as pure, innocent, and beautiful, right?"

"Yes." I nodded. "Then again, considering Julie's just a little girl, it's no wonder she has a pure and innocent aura, is it?"

"Yes and no. There is a smorgasbord of pureness and innocence in terms of aura. Every kid has a different aura, just like adults. By the way, why do you address her as Julie instead of Jules?" Brian asked me, munching on the toast soaked in the egg yolk.

I shrugged. "That's because she informed 'Jules' is a special nickname reserved for her close friends, and she made it clear I wasn't her friend."

"What?" Rick frowned. "I'll have to have a nice chat with her when she's back."

"No, Rowling. You don't have to do that." Brian shook his head, but a corner of his mouth was quirking up. "Let the girl handle her own feelings."

"Um... I'm not quite following?" I said, sounding more like a question than a statement.

"What are you talking about?" At first, Rick seemed to be as clueless as me, but soon he furrowed his eyebrows as if he'd come up with some kind of a theory. "Mandy, don't worry about her attitude. She'll be more than thankful for you when she's back." He squeezed my hand.

"Okay, now let's go back to the main topic." Brian's face turned serious. "The old woman was seen in a black Mercedes with a driver clad in black, right? I often see Aurora at TV stations, and if I recall it right, her secretary's always in black and so are her drivers. Also, she's got five black showy cars, including a Mercedes. The rumor is that Aurora Westwood is notorious for her black magic, like she's used little kids as a tool for attracting not-so-nice spirits."

"Excuse me? Is that like a sacrifice?" I gasped, and Rick glanced again at Julie's photo.

"You can say that," Brian said, looking at

Rick's face. "Still, we're not certain Aurora's the one who abducted Jules, right?"

"Right. Jules is alive," Rick reassured us. "I don't feel that she's hurt or anything."

"Good. Anything else you noticed on Saturday?" Brian pressed on.

"Well...." I recalled the encounter chronologically. "The secretary, I thought I'd met her from somewhere, but I couldn't recall when and where. So I asked her if we've met, and she denied meeting me. I don't know why, but the two moles aligned by the corner of her mouth like a pair of eyes... I think I've seen those moles."

As I knitted my eyebrows, trying to search for clues in my foggy memory, Rick interjected, "What's the secretary's name?"

"It's Ms. Seymour. I don't know her first name. Aurora just called her Ms. Seymour."

"It's Paloma," Brian chimed in. "The secretary's name is Paloma. She's on a first-name basis with the TV producers."

"Paloma Seymour. I've heard that name," Rick muttered, tapping the table with his index finger. Then he turned to me. "You said she has two moles by the corner of her mouth, right?"

"Yes." I nodded.

Rick snapped his fingers. "Now I remember. She's the wife of Ryan Francine. Her name was written in the case file of Jackson Frederick Orchard's murder. So, she went back to her maiden name following the hubby's death."

"Jackie's case file... oh... yes," I muttered,

recalling NYPD's case file that I'd gone through over and over. Ryan Francine was one of the choreographers from the *Aladdin* production Jackie was working on shortly before her death. Francine was noted for his premature death before the NYPD went to ask him more questions. The Paloma I remembered from the case file looked cheerful, but the Ms. Seymour I saw a few days ago had no resemblance to her past portrait. If I recalled it right, her young daughter was also killed in the car accident that killed her husband. It wasn't hard to imagine that having lost both at the same time must have taken a toll on her.

"Anyway, let's focus on Jules for now." Rick looked at the black card from Aurora Westwood. "Why don't we pay her a visit?"

* * *

Forty-five minutes later, I was being led to the spacious salon at Aurora Westwood's mansion. Located in the most upscale neighborhood populated by embassies, consulates, and super-huge mansions, Aurora's property was by far the most intimidating, with secure walls surrounding the two-story building like a fortress.

Paloma Seymour, Aurora's secretary, led the way. Just like the time we'd met at Lincoln Center Theater, the secretary didn't show any kind of emotions and was clad in black from head to toe.

"Ms. Westwood will be so glad to have you over," she said, as we traveled down the long corridor with twists and turns like a maze. "She was looking forward to talking to you."

The corridor was filled with the aromatic scent of a psychic's office—only it smelled more expensive than the average psychic reading room.

"So, Ms. Seymour, how long have you been working for Ms. Westwood?" I asked nonchalantly.

"I've been with her for almost three years," she replied, almost whispering.

"Three years?" I said, thinking that the secretary had started her current job following the death of her husband and daughter.

"Yes." She nodded. Her face was unreadable, but she seemed as if she were observing me as intensely as I did her.

"Wow." I chuckled lightheartedly. "You must have witnessed the most amazing, awe-inspiring miracles during your career with Ms. Westwood."

"No, I haven't." She shook her head slowly. "I don't seem to have sharp perceptions like Ms. Westwood does. Unfortunately, I haven't had a chance to feel the miracle, even when I'm witnessing it from up close." As she said that, a subtle but distinctive emotion crossed her face for the first time. It seemed like a mixture of sadness and loss. There also was desire, perhaps.

When we reached the salon, she told me to make myself comfortable and not to hesitate to call her using the phone on the low table, for she'd always be available when I need anything. She left a tray of tea and assorted petit fours, such as colorful macaroons that looked like jewelry, chocolate truffles, and little cakes.

Looking at the tray full of yummy-looking confections, I had to resist my urge to try one, or two… or three of them. And the sweet, inviting aroma….

Before sending me inside the mansion that looked more like a fortress, Rick and Brian made me swear never to touch, much less eat or drink, anything. I had every intention of sticking to their order. I couldn't recall any fairy-tale characters who had a fun time after eating food served by the evil witch. Okay, so Hansel and Gretel outsmarted the evil witch by conning her and kicking her into the hot oven, but I didn't see an oven nearby, and I didn't have a sidekick.

Speaking of a sidekick, I wondered where Jackie was and how her interview with Tyler went. According to her, finding me was like tuning the radio, and she could find me wherever I was. I'd left a note for her on the dining table at Rick's place, telling her about my visit to Aurora Westwood and the address, hoping extra information would make it easier for her to find me.

I observed the vast, luxurious room while sitting on a cushy beige sofa with Cabriole legs. The place was embellished with Rococo-style furniture, flooded with white and gold, with the occasional peppering of pale blue. I found myself wondering the price of the artworks like the painting on the walls and the vases on the cupboard. I also wondered if one of the vases was a real Ming vase or a replica. That red-and-white vase resembled one I'd seen in a catalog.

Checking the time on my phone for the umpteenth time, I wondered if it was a bad idea to visit here all by myself. Rick, Brian, and I hopped in a Lexus SUV and were heading for the address written on Aurora's black card. At that time, Rick and Brian insisted on accompanying me to the Westwood mansion, but as we got closer, I realized visiting the famous psychic on my own seemed like a better option. Arriving with a hotshot FBI agent and an up-and-coming exorcist in tow would seem like a declaration of war, whereas visiting on my own would appear like a social visit. Though reluctant, Rick and Brian agreed with my suggestion. They were waiting for me in front of the citadel-like mansion.

Having made no appointment prior to this visit, Aurora wasn't in, but that alone didn't bother me. What bothered me big-time was the lack of windows in this room. From the outside, the upscale two-story building looked like a posh gallery, but once inside, I noticed it was more like a dungeon.

Thanks to having been kept in this basement, I was receiving a terrible signal on my phone. I wished I'd brought a paperback, or at least a magazine to kill time.

In an attempt to distract myself from the sweets and to look for Julie—if she was even being kept captive in this dungeon—I stood up and walked to the door, but I had to face the grim situation the moment I opened the door. A woman in a black suit was standing outside of the door. She was tall and her build screamed "Former MMA fighter!"

"Hello? May I help you?" she said. I caught an Eastern European accent in her words. Her lips were formed in the shape of a smile, but there was no humor in her eyes.

"Hi!" I displayed a smile that I hoped to be friendly, trying not to gasp. "Well, I was hoping to visit the powder room."

"I see. The powder room is this way. Let me show you." She nodded and started walking.

Following her in the corridor, a part of me was tempted to run away, except I knew better than to get on Aurora's nerves.

CHAPTER 6

In the meantime, while I struggled—and immediately failed—to navigate in Aurora Westwood's dungeon, Jackie was running her own investigation.

"Hi there! Good morning!" She waved at the ghost of a dead high school student, who was standing at the same place as yesterday. "How are you feeling today?"

"The same as yesterday. I'm dead." Tyler McGraw shrugged. "Where's your friends today?"

"They're meeting someone who makes me a little jittery, so I decided to take some time off and chat with you."

"Wow, can you do that?" The boy ghost widened his eyes.

"Of course. We're friends, and sometimes a girl just needs alone time. For instance, when she's having her intimate moments with her beau, Rick, I don't want to interrupt. I respect her privacy." Jackie winked, grinning.

"Oh yeah? How long have you been stalking her?"

"Stalking? Me? No way!" Jackie flipped her arms dramatically. "Okay, so when I met Mandy for the first time and I sensed her ability to see me, I demanded that she find my killer. But now that I've been sticking around her for over a year, I'm feeling more like a sister and guardian angel. Oh, don't forget

I'm also a good buddy helping her and Rick with their investigations. Unlike living humans, we can sneak into places and eavesdrop without warrants."

"I see. Good for you." The boy ghost nodded, glancing at the wound on Jackie's side. "So, you've been murdered. Did they find your killer?"

"No, not yet." Jackie shook her head sadly. "I often find myself wondering if I want to find my killer that badly. I like hanging around Mandy and Rick, though I can't have direct communication with Rick. I'm unsure what will happen if my murderer is actually caught…. Okay, enough about me. By the way, Mandy and Rick are meeting this exorcist called Brian Powers."

"I've heard his name," Tyler said. "The rumor says he's exorcised ghosts from some of the hottest haunted spots. Is he that strong?"

"He's strong!" Jackie held herself with both arms. "I think he's capable of exorcising me with just a blink of his eyes. His power is, like, totally enormous, and that's why I try not to go near him unless absolutely necessary. Still, I can't help feeling something like holiness coming from him. I think he's a good guy. He has this scary façade, but underneath that, he's hiding his gentle heart."

"A good guy with a gentle heart," Tyler muttered. "Sounds like he's the complete opposite of Aurora Westwood."

"I know! Isn't she like a black hole? Like… capturing everything in the darkness that is hers, never letting them out. Tyler, have you ever met her?"

"Oh no. I just caught the rumors of her." Tyler shook his head. "I'm stuck here, but movable ghosts feed me with rumors when they come across me."

"Uh-huh. By the way, speaking of rumors, the moms in this neighborhood believe you committed suicide."

"What? Me? Killing myself? No way!" Tyler said. For Jackie, it was the first time she'd heard the boy ghost speaking in such a strong tone of voice.

"Of course, I know you didn't kill yourself," Jackie reassured. "I don't feel the loathing and despair from you, unlike the people who'd killed themselves. Then again, people don't normally just fall from the rooftop of the building where they live. After all, you don't look like a former alcoholic or drug addict."

"Um… thanks?" Tyler let out a low chuckle.

"So, what caused your fall?" Jackie asked casually.

"Well…." Tyler knitted his eyebrows. After a pause, he said, "It was an accident. A freak accident."

"How so?" Jackie encouraged.

"I was hanging with my lifelong buddy since kindergarten, Matt Weisberger. Summer break was about to start, and we were a little high on sugar and anticipation for everything. We were just two high school freshmen—totally carefree, mostly thinking about sneaking into preppy bars near NYU and having fun." Tyler took a deep breath. "Then Matt brought up the Susan topic. She's another friend from kindergarten. The three of us had been good buddies… until Susan stole a kiss from me. I didn't and couldn't accept her kiss. I liked her fine, but I couldn't see her as a potential girlfriend. She's like a sister to me, but Matt was offended by the way I rejected her, and he punched me."

"Ouch," Jackie muttered.

"Totally." Tyler agreed. "So I punched him back, telling him I knew he had the hots for Susan and he should have been consoling her instead of assaulting me."

"Wait, that's why you rejected Susan? To give Matt a chance?"

"Yes and no." Tyler shrugged. "I secretly had a crush on him."

"Oh, I see. I know that feeling." Jackie patted the boy ghost on his shoulder, or rather, moved her hand to pretend she was touching him. After all, they were both ghosts and couldn't touch each other.

"We got into an ugly fight, which was unfair. Matt was a quarterback hopeful, and I was a member of debate club! I've seen the presidents of debate clubs with macho physiques and attitude like some kind of MMA fighters at competitions, but unfortunately, I've never been one of them."

"Ooh…."

"I knew it was better to back off rather than keep fighting as a human punching bag, so I jumped over the fence of the rooftop. Of course, dying wasn't in my best interest, and I had every intention of grabbing the railing at the edge of the rooftop. Except, I was much more excited than I thought because my hands were sweaty. And the next thing I knew, I was in the middle of a freefall from the sixth floor. As a result, I'm talking to you just like this." Tyler gave her a shy smile.

"So, it was purely accidental," Jackie said. "What's keeping you here? The curse by a woman scorned?"

"A woman scorned? Are you talking about Susan?" Tyler's eyes widened. "No way, she's not a person who'd hold a grudge against someone."

"Uh-huh. You sound honest, and you don't sound like you resent Matt."

"No, I have nothing against him. It's just...." He frowned. "It's just Matt has to forget about me and go on with his life. I've been dead for over a year, and he's still bringing flowers every month. Can you believe that? As for Susan, she's only visited here twice."

"But it was just an accident, wasn't it?"

"It was. I jumped the fence voluntarily, but he's still trapped with the past, loathing himself, feeling responsible for the accident. So he got scared and ran away, and he couldn't tell anyone about what happened on the day of my death. I don't give a damn about such things, but it's his regrets and sorrow that are keeping me here." Tyler crossed his arms and looked up at the sky.

"What a shame." Jackie shook her head.

"I know. It's unhealthy on all levels. Matt quit football, saying he couldn't just keep on playing like nothing's happened. I told him to quit grieving and blaming himself over and over. The worst part is he can't hear me." Tyler held his head in both hands.

"I know what you mean," Jackie said

sympathetically. "In my experience, less than one percent of people can see us, and even when someone can, they treat us like we don't exist. Mandy is almost like my only contact in this world. I was sad, enraged, panicked, and devastated when I met her for the first time. I'd lost the sense of time, and my sufferings seem to last forever with a capital F."

"You're so fond of that detective."

"Yes, I am. Technically, she's not a detective. She's a special assistant with the FBI. Hey, do you mind if I tell her your story? I have a hunch she'll be able to help you with Matt."

"But the guy—Rick?—he seems very protective of her. Doesn't it bother you?" The boy ghost cocked his head to the side.

"No way!" Jackie chuckled. "I want her to be happy. They're made for each other."

"Okay."

"Right now, their hands are full with a daughter of their good friend being kidnapped, but once Julie's back, I'll tell Mandy about you and Matt. She was worrying about you. Definitely, she's gonna help you."

"About that girl…. She's not coming back," Tyler whispered. Jackie noticed his hands were clenched into fists, trembling.

"Excuse me? Do you recall anything else about Julie?"

"Oh… hell… I'm not supposed to tell this." Frowning, Tyler shook his head. "Actually, Aurora Westwood visited me two days ago."

"What?"

The boy ghost directed his gaze at his loafers, avoiding Jackie's eyes. "I've been asleep most of the time lately, and I was dozing off at that time… but then she talked to me from inside of her car. She spoke to me with a voice that directly echoed into my brain, just like telepathy."

"What did she say?"

"She told me to stay awake for the next day, and make sure that I witnessed a girl getting kidnapped. She also told me to be ready to meet a ghost whisperer lady called Amanda or Mandy. Aurora told me to feed Mandy false information. I told you guys about a black Mercedes and an old lady with heavy makeup, but at that time, I was only feeding you the info Aurora gave me. During the actual kidnapping, the person who snatched the girl was a middle-aged woman driving a white VW."

"Oh my God! Does that mean Aurora Westwood is the one pulling the strings of everything?" Jackie gasped.

"Aurora wasn't in the car during the kidnapping. Perhaps the woman was someone hired by Aurora, or manipulated by her. I was surprised and, at the same time, skeptical about her command, but what could I have done? I couldn't say no to her… I just couldn't. I was scared of her. Whenever a ghost like me doesn't work as she wishes, she sweeps the spirit out of this world, deliberately torturing them forever, maximizing the agony." Tyler bit his lower lip.

"Did she threaten you?" Jackie furrowed her eyebrows.

The boy ghost nodded. "That witch is notorious for manipulating ghosts, using them as her slaves. Every ghost in this town knows that. She even goes so far as to have ghosts possess humans, just for the sake of manipulation. Jackie, you told me you're afraid of Brian Powers, right? It's only natural. You have to be scared of people with the power for exorcism when you're a ghost, but Aurora's power happens to be extra huge."

"But, is that really…?" Jackie was tempted to continue with the word "possible," but then she recalled the overwhelming force she'd felt at the previous encounter with the TV psychic. After that, she had to accept Tyler's story. She was as scared of Aurora Westwood as Tyler was.

"I apologize for feeding you and your friends false information," Tyler said through gritted teeth.

"No worries, it happens all the time," Jackie reassured. "By the way, can you tell me more about the woman in the white car who took Julie away?"

"Of course." Tyler nodded and started talking. Jackie noticed the boy ghost's voice was stronger than ever.

CHAPTER 7

"Ms. Meyer is talking with Ms. Westwood. No, I can't interrupt their meeting for you," replied the voice coming from an intercom on the wall of Aurora Westwood's fortress. "I'm afraid you're wasting your time. I suggest you leave."

"I suggest you let me in," Rick Rowling countered. "No one has ever had fun times by obstructing law enforcement."

"Ms. Westwood is extremely busy, and she cannot meet with anyone without an appointment. I suggest you return another day, possibly with a warrant," she said, and then the line went dead. Despite the seriousness of her words, the voice sounded somehow happy—as if she had found pleasure in rejecting them.

Rick crossed his arms in silence. He didn't say anything, but the bulging veins in his neck made his displeasure obvious. It had been over an hour since Mandy went into the fortress, and she wasn't taking their calls or returning his texts.

"Hey, what are you thinking?" Brian asked.

"What am I thinking? I'm thinking how to destroy this building to ashes *and* rescue Mandy in a good shape," Rick said sarcastically.

"Come on, Rowling. Don't be ridiculous," Brian said. "Aurora Westwood isn't just a phony psychic. She's got pet politicians all over D.C. You have no idea how those old dudes get excited about fortune-telling. Compared to them, high school girls hanging at a fortune-telling café seem like total skeptics." Then he looked midair. "Hey, it's you, Jackie."

"Is she here? What does she say?" Rick demanded, squinting in the direction Brian was looking.

"Hi, Brian, Rick!" Jackie said breathlessly, frantically flipping her arms. "Mayday, mayday! I went to see this boy ghost, Tyler, and he says Aurora Westwood forced him to falsely testify about Julie's kidnapping."

After conveying the ghost's words to Rick, Brian cursed. "Holy shit. I knew the evil witch employed some nasty, crooked tactics about her many predictions and exposing celebrities' dirty laundry, but by enslaving dead people? Talk about crossing the fine line!"

"Don't tell me that Aurora kidnapped Jules just to drag Mandy into her house of horror," Rick said through gritted teeth.

"Don't ask a question with an answer you don't want to know," Brian groaned. "Still, Aurora should know Mandy's with the FBI, and I don't think that old bat will go as far as killing her, but…."

"She won't get away with this. I'll crash that devil before she attempts any dirty tricks on Mandy. It's a promise!" Rick spat.

"Oh my God, what do we do?" Jackie paced in the midair.

"Chill, Jackie," Brian scolded her.

"Jackie." Rick looked at the direction Brian

was glaring at. "Go inside this fortress and tell Mandy to get the hell out of there. You can do that, right?"

"Who? Me?" Jackie gasped. "Well... I mean... I'm not really comfortable getting close to Aurora Westwood, and I feel something like a shield surrounding the walls...."

"Rowling, Jackie here isn't keen on sneaking into the fortress of horror," Brian informed Rick, who glared directly at Jackie despite his inability to see dead people.

"For your information, Jackie"—the veins in his neck were not just visible but pulsating, but Rick's tone of voice was deceptively calm—"if something happens to Mandy, she won't be able to help you find your killer."

The ghost of a drag queen bit her lower lip. "All right, let me try." She charged toward the wall but immediately bounced back.

"Oh shit," Brian muttered. "This building is protected by physical walls and spiritual walls. The spiritual shield deflected Jackie."

"Do something, Brian," Rick barked. "That's what you do."

"Why do I feel I'm being treated like a handyman?" Brian complained, but he took a little silver wand out of his jacket pocket.

"Because basically everyone's a handyman with their own sets of skills." Rick shrugged nonchalantly. "Now get it done already."

Brian shushed him, closing his eyes. Holding the silver wand in his right hand, he directed it at the wall and moved his hand as if he were dowsing for water or something. "Oh... gotcha, but this shield wasn't created by Aurora herself. Hmm... perhaps I can push the door open for a brief while. Rowling, Jackie, step down, ladies!" With a warning peppered with wisecrack, Brian put his hand in his jacket pocket again and took out a white paper craft and a lighter. The card-sized paper was shaped like a human. Brian struck the lighter, igniting the paper craft, and then he threw the burning paper at the wall.

The paper flew in the air with an unexpected velocity, charging ahead like a soldier with its own will. Then the air was audibly buzzing, prompting Rick to take an additional step back and Jackie to shriek.

"There you go, Jackie!" Brian turned to her. "Go inside while the gate is open!"

"Are you serious?" Jackie squawked, looking pale and shaking.

"Jackie, please." Rick begged.

"All right! I will!" Pumping her fists, Jackie charged into the building, screaming, "Geronimooooo!"

* * *

Back in the salon at Aurora Westwood's dungeon, I sighed again. I had counted my sighs after they had reached forty-eight, but then I found myself depressed, so I ditched counting.

Dasha, the security guard outside the salon's door, accompanied my trip to the powder room. I couldn't help wondering if she'd accompany me inside the bathroom. To my relief, she waited outside of the door, but having someone listening to me wasn't very soothing, so I kept on flushing while I did my business. Knowing Aurora's multimillion-dollar empire, my heart didn't ache from shooting up her water bill. I tried to milk information about Julie by befriending Dasha, but unfortunately, she wasn't in the mood to make a new friend.

I checked the time for the umpteenth time, finding I'd been stuck there for over an hour. I seriously started thinking about leaving. The more time that passed, the more my stomach churned with the feeling that I was probably wasting my time. I wished Jackie was with me. In that case, at least, I'd have someone to talk to.

Then, all of a sudden, a drag queen in flashy neon attire jumped in front of me.

"Thank God you're still okay, Mandy!" Jackie shrieked the moment she saw me, flinging herself onto me. Just like usual, her arms went through me without actually touching me, but that time, she seemed extra emotional.

"Wow, I was just thinking about you! Did I just summon you here? Oh my God, I didn't know I could do that!" I gasped. "How did I do that? Did I obtain some kind of a Pokémon master ability or something? I'm getting new skills like every day or what?"

"Um...." Jackie cleared her throat. "Actually, it's Brian who helped me into this godforsaken place of an evil witch's cave. This building is shielded with her power, and he managed to crack a hole in it, and here I am. By the way, you have no idea how Rick's been worried about you."

"Really?" My mood perked up inadvertently as she mentioned Rick.

"Yeah, yeah. Anyway, Mandy, we have to leave here pronto!" Jackie said breathlessly. She should have known about her inability to touch me, but still, she tried to pull my arm as if she was desperate to lead me out of the building.

"You know what? I stumbled upon the truth! It wasn't an old lady in a black Mercedes! Julie was snatched by a middle-aged woman driving a white car instead. Tyler had to feed us false information yesterday because he was threatened by Aurora Westwood to lie to us. Mandy, you were sooo right! Aurora is the one who's been pulling the strings behind Julie's kidnapping."

"Excuse me? So, did she use Tyler in order to mislead the investigation?"

"Yes, but that's only part of the story. Rick and Brian just reached this theory that Aurora Westwood kidnapped Julie in order to get you, and I can't agree more with the boys."

Listening to Jackie's explanation about the sequences of events outside of Aurora's dungeon, my head spun with confusion. Okay, so I would never have set foot in this place if weren't for Julie's kidnapping. Then again, I had a hard time figuring out why the famed and celebrated psychic bothered to lure me to her home.

"Jackie, you mentioned the middle-aged woman who took away Julie had no makeup," I said, thinking. "I think I've met such a person lately, like… Paloma Seymour, Aurora's assistant? Oh my God! If it's really true that Aurora's pulling the strings about everything, then I just can't leave here, can I? You know how worried Julie's parents are about her. I have to stay here and find—"

"No way!" Jackie interrupted. She flipped her arms toward the door. "I know you want to help Dr. Meredith and her hubby, but you don't understand. You're in grave danger right now, and you should really stop dawdling. Aurora Westwood could come in any second, ready to manipulate you with some evil ghosts. Oh, don't tell me you've conveniently forgotten about the time that engineer dude's ghost took over you. I had to literally fly over to Brian and Rick for help!"

"Well, well, well. That is quite a story, isn't it?" Aurora Westwood interjected. Jackie gasped, and I jumped off the sofa. The celebrated TV psychic was emerging into the salon where I'd been kept waiting. I didn't notice the door opening, mostly because it opened without a sound and Aurora didn't bother with knocking. Just like on TV, she was clad in an all-black attire from head to toe, sporting crimson lips and lots of splashy jewelry. When she was on TV, she was totally ageless, but meeting her in person, I presumed her to be around mid-seventies.

"Amanda, my apologies for keeping you waiting here," the psychic said breezily, and then she looked at Jackie. "Oh, look at you, pretty ghost. Hello, dear, what's your name?"

"Um… my name is Jackie," the ghost

responded in a shaky voice.

"Hello, Jackie." Aurora stared at Jackie with an extreme intensity. "I like your necklace. You must be feeling very *festive*."

Jackie froze on the spot, her mouth in an O.

"Jackie, you have to go," I said, trying my best not to wobble while on my feet. "Ms. Westwood and I have something to discuss."

"But, Mandy—" Jackie attempted to argue, but I shushed her.

"Just go. Please."

The ghost of a drag queen pouted, clenching her fists. "Sometimes, I totally, truly wish I could smack your stubborn hard head!" she spat, then disappeared into thin air.

"You're so protective of her, aren't you?" Aurora commented.

"What are you talking about?" I tried to sound nonchalant, though my voice was as shaky as Jackie's.

"You've just let her escape in order to protect her from me." Flashing the scariest smile I'd ever seen, she looked me directly in the eyes.

Instinctively averting my eyes from her gaze, I shrugged. "She's fun to be around, but I'm here strictly for business today. No one needs distractions at a business meeting."

"I see. So, what's your *business* about? Please feel at home and have a seat." Aurora indicated the sofa with the palm of her hand as she sat on a Louis XVI-style chair. As if on cue, Dasha brought a tray with a teapot and two cups.

We sat in silence while Dasha filled the two cups with hot liquid. Hibiscus tea, I assumed. The aroma was sweet yet refreshing, and the color was a strong pink, bordering on blood red. When she was done with serving tea, Aurora gestured for the female security guard to leave.

"So, tell me about the business you were talking about."

"It's about this girl, Julie Grey. I want her back with her parents. She's missing, and I know you had something to do with her disappearance," I said, trying my best to put on a confident look.

"Do you have evidence?" Aurora tilted her head to the side as she took a sip of tea.

I was intimidated by her blasé gesture, but I went on. "I know Ms. Paloma Seymour, your assistant, is the person who abducted Julie." I had no evidence, but considering Paloma wasn't a total stranger to Julie, the secretary had easier access, at least.

"Oh really? Isn't that terrible." Aurora made a face as if she'd just heard the most terrifying thing, but obviously, her reaction was merely a façade. "If so, why don't you arrest Paloma? I couldn't care less," she continued breezily.

"Are you sure?" I asked. "In that case, this place will be thoroughly searched—and I mean every corner." I tried to sound as bold and confident as my counterpart but I wasn't sure if I did it right. I had expected a more dramatic reaction from Aurora, but so far, she was acting as if nothing irregular had happened.

"Whatever. You can search every corner of this humble abode if you have a warrant." She put the teacup back on the tray, a chunky bracelet with a ton of diamonds gleaming on her wrists.

"Oh… really," I mumbled in disappointment. So far, I'd been pushing hard, wishing she'd blurt out something about the kidnapping, but the celebrated psychic in front of me wasn't fazed at all. She didn't deny her secretary's involvement, but at the same time, she didn't admit anything. Then again, my gut instinct was screaming, "It's her!"

After a pause, I said, "Still, if your secretary gets arrested for kidnapping a little girl, you'll be exposed to unwanted attention, possibly with some damage, I imagine."

"Why, Amanda, thank you so much for caring about me." Aurora chuckled, sounding more like the cackle of an evil witch. "In that case, Paloma has to pay—with her own life, perhaps," she continued like she was talking about her plans for replacing a carpet. She didn't sound like she was joking or bluffing.

I opened my mouth and then closed it, just like a suffocating goldfish. At that moment, I knew this famed psychic in front of me was capable of murder without a fraction of remorse. I had no evidence, but I just knew it. She might have even committed a murder or two, using means that couldn't be prosecuted.

Facing the old woman grinning like a cat licking cream—or an evil witch savoring someone else's demise—I resisted the urge to pass out on the spot. I took a deep breath in an attempt to regain my composure. According to the cop shows, the most important thing about kidnapping cases was retrieving the abductee safely. I had to do something.

"Um…." I cleared my throat. "By the way, Ms. Westwood, if we could have Julie back safe and sound, I can make an arrangement so that your name won't be mentioned in regard to the culprit." Okay, so I had no such authority, but I had to say something…anything…. I just couldn't nod to her words like an idiot and leave with no clue about Julie's whereabouts.

"Oh my goodness! Are you trying to bargain with me?" Aurora cracked up laughing.

"Excuse me, but that wasn't supposed to be a punchline," I pointed out, prompting the star psychic's face to turn serious.

"You intrigue me so much," she said, looking into my eyes. "Look at the colors of your aura. Are you aware of your aura changing its color every moment, as if it's revolving?" The old woman's eyes flickered with a devilish gleam.

"No," I mumbled, trying to look away, but somehow my gaze was captured by her deep, cold, ice-blue eyes that sparkled with dusky shades of purple.

After a somewhat lengthy staring match, Aurora muttered, "Fine."

"What do you mean?" I drew back from her, startled. Whatever she was referring to, it shouldn't have been "fine."

"I'm open to arranging that little girl—Julie?—to return home in a very good shape." The words she uttered were something I wasn't expecting.

"Are you sure?" My ears and, of course, my mood perked up. For a moment, I regretted determining Aurora as evil. Perhaps she might have been nice, soft, and fluffy at the bottom of her heart.

But then she continued. "Under one condition."

"Which is?" I gulped, feeling uneasy. Despite my previous regret, I hadn't fully ditched the theory of Aurora Westwood being an evil witch, and in fairy tales most villains tended to demand a few decades of your life-span in return to what you want. Call me a self-centered egomaniac, but I wasn't keen on trading my decades of life expectancy with the girl who didn't even regard me as her friend.

"Oh, don't worry, Amanda. All you have to do is promise to work for me."

"Excuse me?" I frowned. "You mean, like, working as your maid?" *Should I mention that I had a full-time job?* I wondered.

"Oh no. I already have the best people as my domestic help and I'm not recruiting for now. I'm offering you a position with much higher potential. You can keep your job with the FBI while working for me. If I'm truly satisfied with your work, I can even push you up to the director of the FBI," the TV psychic said breezily. "Imagine becoming the first female head of the FBI."

My jaw dropped. I looked at her carefully, suspecting she was cracking a horribly lame joke. Obviously, Aurora didn't know me. So far, I'd had offers to be promoted into a special agent from a special assistant, but I had declined all of them. Considering my track record of clumsiness, the chances of me passing the physical exams were nonexistent. Oh, did I mention I couldn't read auras or exorcise the dead spirits? I could easily imagine Rick Rowling leading the FBI—though he tended to be a tad bit too adventurous and blasé for other people's feelings, but he was improving!—but yours truly being mounted as the head of the FBI was the stupidest idea ever.

"Excuse me, but I'm not fit for the role, I'm afraid. I love this country, and I don't want to put America in jeopardy because of my clumsiness. Someone more suitable should be responsible for running the domestic intelligence and security of the United States," I said. I was using my clumsiness as an excuse, but I didn't mention my bigger concerns. Actually, the reason I didn't want to be the head of the FBI was my past of being falsely accused of being the Grim Reaper, and I still felt uneasy shaking hands with other people. In my previous life as a medical student I'd witnessed three people dropping dead just minutes after touching me in three consecutive days. I'd love to say that I'd left that dark history behind, but when you're the head of the FBI, you have to shake hands with many supposedly "important" people, and I didn't want to take chances. What if one or more of the *important* people dropped dead in front of the TV cameras? I didn't know what triggered people to die on me, but I knew the media wouldn't just shrug it off as an irregular incident.

"You don't understand." She clicked her

tongue. "You won't be running the show. I will. Besides, you will be my asset. By utilizing you as my puppet, I'll be able to obtain your power as well as take the FBI under my control. Talk about killing two birds with one stone."

Listening to her talking about me like a tool or an item in her stupid video game, I genuinely felt like bitch-slapping her, but I didn't. The evil witch in front of me hadn't fessed up about Julie's whereabouts, and she didn't look like the kind of a person who'd turn the other cheek when her right cheek had been hit. Still, I had to make my point. "May I suggest something? Even with your assistance, the chances of my obtaining a high-rank position at the FBI are slim to none. Isn't it better if you *utilize* someone with more potential of becoming the director of the FBI, or someone at a very high rank?"

That time, Aurora chuckled. "That is none of your business. I know how to do my job," she said matter-of-factly, as if she had already been getting ready to take the FBI over. To my horror, she didn't sound like she was joking. Of course, she couldn't have been joking. According to Brian, the celebrated psychic had already taken possession of multiple politicians and bureaucrats. I could easily imagine her turning some of them into enthusiastic believers using predictions. Also, it wasn't difficult to imagine her blackmailing politicians and bureaucrats for scandals. Considering she'd been using dead people as informants, digging up anyone's dirty laundry should be a piece of cake for her.

As I knitted my eyebrows, she looked into my eyes again. "Amanda, I don't quite understand your hesitancy for becoming the first female director of the FBI. Why is that? Are you playing the dumb card, or are you afraid you might lose your boss's interest if you outranked him?"

CHAPTER 8

I almost flinched as Aurora mentioned my boss out of the blue.

"What do you know about my boss?" I asked cautiously.

"What do I know? Aside from well-known facts about him being the heir to USCAB and his name being listed in the top ten of the most eligible bachelors in New York City multiple times? Well, let me see…." She closed her eyes. "For example, I know he cares about you, choosing to have his leg crashed by a bookcase rather than watching you get hurt by the temper tantrum inflicted by a deranged ghost. I'm glad his leg has healed nicely."

"What?" My jaw dropped. Aurora was talking about an accident last summer in which Rick ended up breaking his leg when he tried to save me. But only a few people in our closest inner circle knew the details of his injury, especially about the part with the ghost. I was talking to a murder victim who became agitated during the interview, and she decided to throw a heavy bookcase at me. Rick didn't mention the part about the ghost even to Meredith, his doctor. "How do you know that?" I gasped.

"Oh, look at you! The shock on your face. Surprised? Did I mention I'm Aurora Westwood?" The old woman grinned. "Mind you, I can talk to dead people just like you."

I knew Aurora could talk to ghosts, but still,

learning that she had so much information about me was a shocker. "Did you hear about the incident from Ellie Hochman?"

In fact, that ghost had been bugging me for months. Generally, ghosts could talk to me, but touching me or throwing objects at me were beyond their means. Still, the ghost of Ellie Hochman managed to strangle me and shove a bookcase full of books at me. When I asked the ghost how she did it, she disappeared suddenly, even though she was at least trying to answer my question. In retrospect, Ellie seemed to have been forcibly removed by someone—like Aurora Westwood, for example. Then again, if Aurora had been pulling strings for Ellie's outburst, followed by her later vanishing, it was only natural that the famed psychic knew *everything* about it. Except, I couldn't think of her motive.

I felt uneasy sitting in front of Aurora. It would have made it easier if I could just ask her, but I didn't know how. I wasn't even sure if it was appropriate to casually ask, "By the way, did you try to hurt me by using a ghost? Did you get rid of her before she fessed up about her relationship with you?"

But before I opened my mouth, Aurora said, "Yes. She regretted her temper and the fact that she'd hurt your boss." She chuckled. "She was shocked by her sudden gain of power. Perhaps you already know it, but normally, ghosts can't physically touch or move objects. The only reason she came across her power was by meeting me. I blessed her with a small amount of power that was to be fueled by her negative emotions. And I say, she was so full of antagonistic feelings."

"Excuse me?" My eyebrows shot up. "Did you deliberately hurt my boss?"

"Oh no. It was my way of greeting you, Amanda," she said nonchalantly. "But your boss interrupted me. I didn't expect that, but he saved you. He cares for you so much. Good for you. I'm jealous."

"Hello? Did you just say that you attempted to hurt me but ended up hurting my boss instead?" I spat, feeling my blood boiling with anger. "How dare you do that to us! What are you, a psycho?"

"Haven't you got any sense of humor? It's all about perspectives. You can thank me for being a cupid. So, he was hurt by a little collateral damage, but if not for his injury you wouldn't be dating him, would you?" The psycho witch shrugged, looking like a cat playing with a mouse.

"But… I didn't ask you to do that!" I snapped. "Do you have any idea how much pain he went through? I would never have asked you to hurt him, and you've just admitted that it was actually your failed attempt to hurt me! Why are you sounding so patronizing, as if you did me some favor? How could you invite me to work for you after all you've done to us? Are you insane, or should I interpret this as a sign of dementia?" My tone sounded bitchy but I didn't care. I was feeling more than defensive and I had every right to be angry.

Aurora snorted. "Anyway, now that you know what I'm capable of, I suggest you accept my offer and start working for me."

"Are you joking? If so, that's not even funny." I shook my head. Actually, I was infuriated about the evil psychic hurting Rick, and I could go on a rant for hours about that, but I wasn't stupid enough to blurt out my potential weakness to my enemy.

So I stood up to leave. "Looks like I've wasted a long time here. Obviously, you have no interest in helping the kidnapped little girl return to her parents. By the way, I'm not interested in accepting your condition to enslave myself in exchange for Julie. I was so stupid to visit you in the first place. This conversation is over, and I'm not thankful for your time." Okay, so I didn't have a clue about Julie's whereabouts, and I wanted to find her, but I couldn't stand another second being stuck with Aurora.

As I started walking, Aurora opened her mouth. "Amanda, don't be so shortsighted. Think about the wealth of information I'll be providing you once you're on my team."

"For your information, I don't want to join your team." Without stopping, I passed by her side.

"Oh really?" she said sarcastically. "For starters, I can tell you something about your ghost pal, Jackie, formerly known as Jackson Frederick Orchard."

My ears perked up at the mention of Jackie's name, but I kept walking... albeit a little slower.

She went on. "I can give you the name of his—or should I say her?—killer, and of course, I'll give you the evidence for the murder."

That time, she grabbed my attention. A smarter woman would have kept walking to make her point, and a lesser woman would have returned to the evil witch, panting like a dog awaiting his treat. I stopped walking. Then I turned back… or at least, I tried to turn back, but somehow one of the tips of my shoes got caught in nothing and I stumbled. In an attempt to avoid falling and embarrassing myself, I put one foot in front of me and then the other while flapping my arms like a chicken trying to fly.

As a result, I literally ran back to her, except my gait was more like a bumble rather than an intentional run.

"Aaaah! I can't stop!" I shrieked, falling toward the evil witch who responded with merely a snicker while I dove onto the very chair where Aurora was sitting.

Thanks to taking many steps during my stumble, I'd managed a soft landing. Also, Aurora somewhat caught me in her arms. "Oh, thank God you caught me," I said, detaching myself from her embrace.

"You already owe me some work, I believe," she said matter-of-factly, but then she grimaced, clutching her head. "What did you do to me?" she demanded, holding her head in both arms.

"What do you mean? I didn't do anything," I replied, puzzled. Personally, I wanted to ask her what she'd done to me so far. Although, considering her track record of messing with my life, I wasn't sure if learning about all her dirty tricks would make me happy. "So, about Jackie's murderer? Who killed her?" I asked, assuming the old witch was faking an ailment, but….

"My head… my head…." Still holding her head, as if she had a monster headache, she started panting like a cow in heat. She was also turning purple—no, pukey puce seemed like a more appropriate term to describe her color. Even with her heavy makeup, she was turning puce.

"Um… are you okay?" I asked, but then she was spewing foam out of the corners of her mouth. Yikes. I wondered if she needed CPR, but I opted out. After all, she was drooling, and I wasn't big on touching her drool. If I were to list something positive about the catastrophe in which I got kicked out of medical school without a degree but with a humongous student loan, it would be getting rid of the risks of touching other people's bodily fluids in line of my job.

Still, as a former medical student, I decided to do something helpful for her—or at least, I tried. "Are you oka—eek!" When I contemplated if I should at least attempt to take her pulse even though I wasn't keen on doing that, I shrieked. The glittering bracelet I'd recognized earlier had disappeared, replaced by a dozen black, furry spiders the size of golf balls. "Wahhh!" I shrieked at the top of my lungs.

"What's happened?" The door burst open and Dasha ran into the salon.

"Auro—I mean, Ms. Westwood has just collapsed, and the spiders…."

"Oh, Madame! Madame Aurora!" Dasha scurried to the TV psychic now practically convulsing. "Madame, are you all right?" She reached for Aurora's arm.

"Excuse me, but perhaps you don't want to touch the spiders. They might be poisonous," I mumbled, but the security guard looked at me as if I'd said something really stupid.

"Are you on drugs or something?" She frowned. "Where are the spiders?"

When I looked at Aurora's arm again, the spiders were gone and there was the bracelet. Still, the diamonds seemed to have lost their previous sparkle. "No… it's just… I was a little panicked. Never seen someone getting so sick so suddenly," I mumbled.

Okay, to tell the truth, someone touching yours truly and collapsing in total agony was actually déjà vu to me, but I wasn't going to share that with the scary security guard. Also, I didn't want to admit my past of being called the Grim Reaper.

I glanced at the purple-colored woman. She was groaning and sweating profusely, looking even worse than a few minutes before.

"Does she have any existing conditions? Like heart disease?" I asked Dasha, just to fill the awkward silence.

"No. She was totally healthy." Dasha shook her head, then reached for the phone on the table and immediately called 911. Once she was done with the dispatcher, she started loosening her employer's clothes, almost barking, "Madame, please look at me. Look at me! Stay with me, stay with me! You'll be fine. Stay with me!"

Watching her trying to resuscitate Aurora, I half expected—and half wished—that it was all a prank and Aurora would get up, shrieking, "Surprise!" Then everyone would laugh their ass off—until I started whacking Aurora and Dasha really hard in their faces. I'd been working diligently for the past few years trying to sweep away being the Grim Reaper. Also, it was my first time to actually witness someone who yelled "Stay with me! Stay with me!" like a cop show character whose partner/lover had just been gunned down.

Talk about a surreal situation....

Even though I wasn't a huge fan of Aurora Westwood, I wished she wouldn't die. I knew I didn't kill her, and the rational part of me was screaming, "People just don't die from touching someone else!" Still... considering my past, I wasn't sure of anything.

When paramedics appeared in the salon, carrying a stretcher, the renowned TV psychic was unconscious, and I answered their questions on autopilot.

"When she was speaking with me, she suddenly clutched her head, saying she had a headache, and then she collapsed. No, she didn't seem to be ill before that. It all happened so abruptly, and...." I felt light-headed as I spoke.

"Miss, relax. Take a deep breath," one of the paramedics said, sitting by my side and patting my hand.

"I-I-I... thought she was having a subarachnoid hemorrhage or something...." Babbling, I watched the paramedic guy in horror, fearing he'd start to break down in agony as his hand touched mine.

"I see. Thank you." When he got up without any signs of sickness, I let out a sigh of relief.

Following Aurora being carried out on a stretcher with Dasha tagging along with the paramedics, I noticed Paloma Seymour, the secretary, wasn't around.

"Excuse me?" I whispered to one of the maids walking along the long corridor. "May I speak to Ms. Seymour?"

"Ms. Seymour?" The maid looked at me as if I'd said something stupid. "She left early, saying she wasn't feeling well."

I thanked her and went out of the extravagant entrance after the paramedics.

* * *

"Let us in! It might be my partner needing the ambulance! If anything, and I mean *anything*, happens to her, you're in big trouble. This is a promise, not a threat." When I came out of Aurora Westwood's mansion, Rick was practically yelling at Aurora's staff at the gate.

"Um… Rick?" I called his name sheepishly, making a little finger wave at him and Brian.

"Mandy!" Rick ran to me and scooped me up in a bear hug. "Are you okay? Nothing hurts?"

"Umm… I'm… good," I gasped. In his strong embrace I recalled that his Calvin Klein model-worthy body wasn't just for the show but actually was armored with hard muscles.

"Are you sure nothing hurts?"

Rick kept on clutching me until Brian said, "Rowling, why don't you stop squishing her so she can breathe?"

"Fine. I'm glad you're okay." Releasing me from his embrace, Rick glanced at the stretcher being loaded into the ambulance. "If you're okay, who's on that?" He arched an eyebrow.

"That's Aurora Westwood," I said.

"Seriously? What happened?"

"Why does she look so… purple?" Brian asked.

"It's complicated." I bit my lower lip as Rick and Brian peppered me with questions. "It was an accident. I was falling toward her, having stumbled on nothing, and she caught me. All of a sudden, she started complaining of a headache, and the next thing I knew, she was convulsing and spewing foam out of her mouth," I mumbled.

Rick and Brian exchanged glances. Thanks to the ambulance blasting its siren, crowds started to gather on the sidewalk.

"Let's leave this place." Rick threw the car key to Brian, took my hand, and led me toward the parked car.

CHAPTER 9

As we got in, I started explaining what had happened inside Aurora Westwood's fortress. I told them how she demanded I be her puppet, and about my fury when she said that she'd hurt Rick using the ghost of Ellie Hochman.

"I was so furious, and I totally, absolutely hated her guts, so I stood up to leave. Then she mentioned she was open to telling me about Jackie's killer, with evidence and everything. I suspected she might have been lying, but at the same time, that piece of information sounded too good to pass up, so I turned back to her. Then one of my shoes caught up with something, or nothing, on the floor, and I fell toward her. I'd managed a soft landing, and she caught me in her arms, but…." I took a deep breath.

"She started turning purple, complaining of a severe headache, collapsing," Rick muttered. "Hmm, why does it sound like déjà vu?"

"Hey, I don't want to hear the G-word," I warned.

"You mean Grim Reaper? No, I'm not saying that word." Rick raised an eyebrow.

"You just did!"

"Don't worry, it's not like every person drops dead after touching you." Sitting on the back seat, Rick patted my arm.

"Yeah, right," Brian chimed in. "I saw Meredith touching her hand on Saturday, and she didn't seem affected."

"Still, I'd really hate to be the direct reason for her death."

"Hey, I'm gonna throw a huge thank-you party if that evil witch ends up dead, and I'm not alone," Brian said in a cheerful tone. "Rumor says she even takes assassination gigs, using curses or black magic or whatever crap."

"I see." Rick nodded. "Considering your track record of killing murderers and rapists who slipped out of the justice system, Aurora certainly falls in the category of people whom you can kill without trying."

"I didn't kill anybody!" I smacked his arm, my voice sounding like Minnie Mouse. I thought Dorothy from *The Wizard of Oz* would have felt the same way as I did when the munchkins thanked her for killing the Wicked Witch of the East. Though in the movie, Dorothy had obviously killed the witch with her family's house.

Rick held my hand. "Anyway, thanks for getting even with Aurora for me. After all, considering the old witch broke my ankle, she deserves a hospital visit."

"That's not the point. I was close to getting to the truth, or at least I felt so. Oh my God, I feel like a total loser." I sighed, my hand still held in Rick's firm grip. "I should have avoided touching her until she'd fessed up about Jackie's killer at least. Also, she hinted that Julie's kidnapper was Paloma Seymour, but she was unconscious at the time when I tried to obtain more information about her. Also, when I tried to speak to Paloma before leaving Aurora's, it turned out she'd gone, taking a sick day."

"Speaking of Paloma Seymour, we're going after her," Rick said nonchalantly. "About ten minutes before the ambulance came in, we saw the secretary coming out of the side entrance." The car was heading for Midtown.

"By the way, Mandy, you should have seen Rowling freaking the hell out when you didn't return from the evil witch's fortress for over an hour." Brian snapped his fingers. "I've never seen him asking for a favor from NYPD."

"Shut up, Brian." Rick snorted. "I didn't ask favors from anyone. It's just Chief DeLaurentis kindly offered to send us some backup manpower."

"Easy, pal. The plainclothes officers you borrowed from NYPD came in handy to have Paloma Seymour tailed." Brian chuckled.

"Oh, I was worried we might have lost her. By the way, I didn't know Ms. DeLaurentis had been promoted," I said. The last time we'd worked with her, she used to be a captain. "Where's Jackie?"

"She's gone back to that ghost boy, Tyler, to clarify if the kidnapper's physical description matches Paloma Seymour. Is that right, Brian?"

"Yeah, that's right." Brian nodded in affirmation.

"Oh," I mumbled.

Rick massaged my forehead with the tips of his fingers. "Stop worrying. At least stop frowning," he said. "Aurora is crooked, and crooked people never hesitate to lie. Just because she said she knew

Jackie's killer doesn't mean she was telling the truth. She might have been just trying to get to you, wanting to capture you in her web."

"You have a point." I nodded. "Speaking of webs, I saw her bracelet dissolving into a dozen of huge, ugly spiders with hairy legs. I know what I'm saying is silly, and I myself am having trouble believing that it really happened. I might have been hallucinating or something, I guess."

"No, you weren't hallucinating, Mandy," Brian said. "I saw Aurora hanging out with a black spider the size of a Chihuahua. That grossed me out, though normally, people don't see them."

"Forget about Aurora. We'll find Jackie's killer with or without her help." Rick wrapped his arm around my shoulders and pulled me close to him.

"Wow, isn't that so very reassuring to hear?" Just like always, Jackie popped up from out of nowhere, moving her arms like she was wrapping them around my shoulders.

"Jackie!" I gasped. I pondered if I should inform her about my conversation with Aurora, but I opted out. After all, Aurora went unresponsive before giving me the killer's name, and she could have been lying about knowing Jackie's killer in the first place.

"Is she back?" Rick tilted his head to the side.

"Yes." I nodded. Then I turned to Jackie. "Hey, I was worried you might not be able to find us while we're moving."

"Come on, girlfriend. I'm your guardian angel. I can find you wherever you are, but Aurora Westwood did somehow jam your aura when you were in her fortress." As the ghost replied, her 'FESTIVE' necklace sparkled. "By the way, I spoke to Tyler, and he testified Julie's kidnapper had two moles lined up at the corner of her lips. Also, the parts about having dark hair peppered with gray strands and having no makeup matched." She touched the right corner of her mouth.

"Good." I nodded, wishing Tyler McGraw was a living human who could testify. If so, we would have been ready to arrest Paloma.

Rick's phone beeped.

"Uh-huh. Got it. Thanks. I'll be there right away." Disconnecting, Rick said, "Hurry up, Brian. It looks like Paloma's decided on her destination."

"Roger that." The exorcist revved the engine.

* * *

We went into one of the buildings at a medical center close to FDR Drive, following the direction provided on the phone call. We met two NYPD officers in plain clothes at the lobby of the trauma center.

The place was crowded with visitors, and I spotted Paloma Seymour among them. She was clad in the same black pantsuit she was sporting at the mansion.

"The staff at Aurora Westwood's place said she was sick, not wounded," I muttered to myself. Also, considering we'd learned about Paloma's destination while we were still in the car, she had been staying in the lobby for quite a long while.

Without stopping at the reception, Paloma walked toward the elevator that led to the ward. Keeping some distance, we followed her.

"Obviously, she's not here to seek medical attention," Rick commented. "Perhaps she's visiting someone in the ward."

"I doubt it. She's not carrying anything that looks like a gift," I said.

As we watched, Paloma wandered about in the elevator hall, like she wasn't sure about her destination. Even from the distance, she looked distracted—absent, even. According to the officers who tailed her to the hospital, she seemed to have had a hard time reaching the facility. For some unknown reason, she didn't immediately enter the hospital and spent quite some time loitering around the entrance.

So far, Paloma had let the elevator go past to the upper floors three times.

I looked up at Brian. "Well, for me, it looks like she's affected by something."

"She's affected? Of course she's affected. That's the understatement of the year." The exorcist crossed his arms. "Even from this distance, I can see at least a dozen spirits tagging along with her. I'd call it a miracle if that doesn't make her gaga."

"Are those spirits manipulating her? Did they come from Aurora Westwood?" Rick asked.

"I don't know where they came from, as they don't have ID tags or anything on them. They might have found her without the old witch's help. But one thing I'm sure of, she's not in a good shape."

As we whispered, Paloma finally realized the

elevator had arrived once more, and that time, she got inside. Thanks to missing three already, Paloma was alone on the elevator.

"I'm going with her to see where she's going." Jackie followed Paloma to the elevator to keep us from losing her. I did a little finger wave that only Jackie could see. The plainclothes officers were still with us, and they should have known about Brian's skillset as an exorcist; however, I assumed they weren't ready to learn about my ghost friend.

When the metal elevator doors closed, we watched the number on the floor indicator. When it stopped at the thirty-eighth, the top floor, we hopped on the next arriving elevator.

When we were just about to reach the thirty-eighth floor, I caught Jackie's shriek. "Hey! Stop it! What do you think you're doing?"

I looked at Brian, who grunted, "We've got to hurry up," through his clenched teeth.

The moment the elevator doors opened, we ran out to the corridor. In front of the elevator was the reception desk, but the receptionist denied having any visitors for the past ten minutes.

"The rooftop!" Brian said sharply, running toward the emergency staircase in the corner of the corridor. Rick, the officers, and I followed the exorcist.

As I went out on the deserted rooftop, a strong breeze sprung up from the East River. I caught sight of metal containers and railings.

"Come quick! She's over there!" Jackie pointed at the woman in black crawling up the railing toward the edge of the building. "You have to do something. She's gonna jump!" The ghost of a drag queen was practically screaming.

"Paloma, stop!" Brian barked, but Aurora Westwood's secretary was unresponsive. As the men darted toward her, she got over the railing, breathing heavily as she reached the edge of the building.

Paloma Seymour was just one step to her death. The NYPD cops ran fast.

"Easy, ma'am," one of them talked to her in a calm voice. "For whatever reasons, jumping off this building to end your life is never the answer."

She was silent for a while, but then she snapped. "What do you know about me? Whether I live or die, it's none of your business!"

No matter what she said, she was talking, and I found it a good sign. She seemed likely to go on a rant and then relax a little—or at least, that was the scenario I was expecting.

And then, all of a sudden, she jumped off the railing toward the inside of the rooftop, charging at the officers. The cops attempted to catch her, but with her unexpected speed and power, she dodged them and came running straight toward me.

At first, I thought she was going to the other side of the rooftop to jump, but instead, she was charging at me.

"Mandy, run!"

"Be careful! This woman isn't herself. She's dangerous!"

I caught Rick and Brian shouting while they ran after Paloma.

"Hey, get a grip! You don't want to do that. You'll regret it!" Jackie was also trying to stop the secretary, but she didn't seem to hear any of the ghost's words and kept on charging toward me.

I started running, but I was never good at it. I heard the middle-aged woman roaring like a wild beast as she came after me. From the corner of my eye, I saw the cops drawing their guns, trying to aim at Paloma, except I happened to be in the possible line of fire.

I really, truly hated this situation.

I hated running away from my attacker, and I especially hated the part about the fear of getting caught. Rick was coming to rescue me, but I had a hunch the deranged Paloma might be stronger than anybody and could possibly hurt him. And of course, I truly, absolutely hated getting hit by stray bullets. Okay, so sometimes I daydreamed about losing some of my extra fat cells, but having them nicked by lead bullets with the possibility of hemorrhaging and infection wasn't high on my to-do list.

So, instead of the running option, I turned back to face her, and without a split second of hesitation, I bitch-slapped her. It came out of impulse, touched with a little bit of calculation. Considering what had happened when I touched Aurora Westwood, I speculated that I might have some chance of winning.

And I was right.

I felt a jolt of electricity the moment I touched her, and Paloma recoiled. "Ahh!" she shrieked, clutching her face.

"I know you've kidnapped Julie" I slapped her again. "Where is she? Tell me! Now!" And I slapped her again.

With a beastly groan, she collapsed onto the gray concrete floor, but I was on a roll.

"Where's Julie? Tell me! In ten seconds, you'll start turning purple and convulsing! Tell me before you die!" I sat on her, pinning her to the floor, and kept shouting like an infuriated version of Natalia Boa Vista from *CSI: Miami* until…

"Mandy, you can stop assaulting her." Rick came and scooped me off the floor.

"It's not an assault. It's an interrogation," I retorted, but Rick was clutching me and I couldn't move.

"Easy," Brian said, then approached Paloma sprawled on the floor. He took out a cross and patted her with it.

After a while, Paloma Seymour coughed with a whoosh of air and she sat up. "Wh-what am I doing here?" she gasped. As she noticed she was on the rooftop of a tall building, she squinted, muttering, "What was I thinking?"

"You just tried to… mmm—" Rick shut me up with a hand over my mouth.

"I believe you've been to this hospital before," Rick said. The tone of his voice was uncharacteristically soft, considering he was dealing with a kidnap suspect who'd attempted to assault me.

Looking around herself, Paloma gasped. "Is it… the hospital where my daughter perished?"

"Yes, it is." Rick nodded. "Your husband was driving the vehicle with your daughter, Annette, and had a car wreck. Is that right?"

"Are you with… NYPD? Did I see you at the funeral?" Paloma asked in a whisper.

"No, I'm with the FBI, and I wasn't at your daughter and husband's funeral. But I know a former NYPD detective who was there," Rick replied. "I also happen to be a close friend of Dr. Grey."

When he mentioned the name Grey, Paloma's pale face contorted.

"Dr. Grey has a daughter named Julie, who's missing. Her parents are crazy with worry and we're looking for Julie. According to a boy who witnessed the kidnapping, the suspect was a slim, middle-aged woman driving a white VW. Do you know anything about the girl's whereabouts?"

Paloma opened her mouth, her lips trembling. "Ah… I… I…."

Brian chimed in. "Paloma, you can trust this guy. And I know you were forced to do so under Aurora Westwood's control. I can testify for you."

"No. No, no, no!" Paloma shook her head violently. "Ms. Westwood never made me do anything."

"In that case, are you saying some stray spirits manipulated you into kidnapping the girl?" Brian furrowed his bushy eyebrows. "You'll have a hard time convincing the jury with that version."

"No… I mean…." Paloma's lips quivered as if she had something to tell but couldn't find the courage to do so.

"Paloma, you've got to—" Brian started lecturing, but Rick shushed the exorcist with a wave of his hand.

"Ms. Seymour, what did it feel like when you lost your only daughter?" he asked bluntly.

Brian took a deep breath. Jackie gasped by my side. "Seriously, Rick?" she said, flapping her arms. "Talk about adding insult to injury!"

I watched Paloma shaking, fearing that she'd try another attempt at ending her life.

She clenched her fists, biting her lower lip. Then she opened her mouth. "Everything's my fault," she said through gritted teeth. "After meeting Julie, Madame Aurora mentioned Annette would be her age... if only she were still alive. I don't know what got into me, but after meeting that beautiful girl, I couldn't stop thinking about her. And the next thing I knew, I... I had this desire to own her... as my child... as if having her would replace my deceased daughter. I don't know how such a monstrosity of an idea got in me, but... but I... took her.... I'm so sorry!" Apologizing profusely, she knelt on ground floor.

I felt Rick's muscles tense as he clenched his hands into fists, but his voice was quiet. "Where is she?"

"She's in a junior suite at the Plaza," Paloma said. "I don't know why, but she's been like a doll. She's seemed somewhat absent for the whole time, and she's unharmed."

"I see. The hotel's close to here. Hey, Brian, can you go to the hotel with the officers so Jules won't be frightened?" Rick turned to the backup officers. "You guys head there immediately with my associate and place the victim in protective custody."

The officers nodded at his command and left with Brian in tow.

CHAPTER 10

When Brian and the officers were gone, Rick immediately made a call to Dr. Meredith Grey. Asking her to put him on speakerphone, he briefed Julie's parents and the agents from both USCAB and the FBI about the turn of events. Then he called the investigation headquarters and arranged a pickup for Paloma as a prime suspect.

In the meantime, I was told by him to keep an eye on Paloma. Watching her in silence like a prison guard was awkward, so I decided to talk to her.

"By the way, Ms. Seymour…."

The woman who had just admitted kidnapping Julie Grey shook her shoulders as if she was terribly startled.

"I'm sorry… so sorry," she mumbled, sobbing.

For a split second, I thought about consoling her, saying things like "It's okay," but I didn't, mostly because I couldn't find anything okay about abducting a child. So I said, "By the way, an actor named Jackson Frederick Orchard was murdered about five years ago."

Jackie, who had been floating by my side the whole time, sucked in air. I looked at her, mouthing, "She might know something about you," and the ghost nodded with a thumbs-up.

"The victim's friends used to call *her* Jackie, and by that I mean she preferred to be addressed as a female. So Jackie attended the Pride Dance party at Pier 26 and met her premature demise on the way home. Ms. Westwood said she knew something about this murder, and I was wondering if you'd heard about it from your employer."

As I spoke, Paloma's hands were visibly shaking. "I… well…," she mumbled.

"You know something, don't you?"

Paloma bit her lower lip in silence for a while before shutting her eyes and then opening them. Finally, she said, "The killer was Ryan Francine, my deceased husband."

Jackie gasped, and so did I. "Excuse me? Before Jackie's murder, there were two murders and an attempted murder. So, do you mean Ryan used this unknown serial murderer as his cover-up to kill his coworker, Jackie?" I asked.

"No." Paloma shook her head. "Ryan… my husband was the serial murderer."

"What?" Jackie and I said in unison, though Paloma didn't seem to sense the ghost of a drag queen.

"Still, according to a witness, the assailant was a young man, probably in his twenties… and he had beard. Your deceased husband was already in his forties back then, wasn't he?" Rick chimed in.

Before Jackie's murder, a total of three victims—two women and a transgender woman—were slashed with a sharp blade close to Pier 26, and it was believed that the series of assaults were committed by the same culprit. One of the victims, an accountant, survived, and thanks to her testimony, the

NYPD had a relatively clear description of the assailant's physical features. According to the testimony, the assailant's height was between 5'8" and 6'. He was chubby with a flabby tummy, clad in a black tracksuit, sporting a beard covering half of his face and a pair of shades.

Ryan Francine was one of the choreographers of the *Aladdin* production, which Jackie played the part of Genie in until she met her untimely demise. I had seen the photo of Ryan Francine, but he didn't match any of the given description. He was muscular but slim, and he didn't have beard.

"I found a bloodstained knife and tracksuit, as well as a fake beard and sunglasses," Paloma said between sobs.

"Oh my…." My jaw dropped.

"Oh, and there were bloodied sweatshirts. Perhaps he'd stuffed them around his waist to obtain a puffy look," Paloma went on. "He was always adamant about banning anyone else visiting his home studio, and… I didn't know why! Okay, so I suspected that he was hiding something from me— such as seeing other women—and I had to check out his studio. But I… I should never have set foot in there. My nosiness won over his ban. Seriously, I could imagine finding something like toothbrushes in feminine colors or sultry lingerie… but I'd never expected coming across what I saw."

I opened my mouth and then closed it. Considering that the assaults took place in dark places at nighttime, the age and body shape could have been easily mistaken. Besides, the witness was practically bleeding her guts out, and when you're bleeding to near death, you wouldn't be thinking straight.

"When I found those bloody items in his closet, I realized my husband was the serial killer by the pier. At that time, two people were killed and the third victim was fighting for her life... TV, newspaper... the media was practically running field days about the serial murderer, and even I could easily put two and two together." She covered her face with both hands.

"You could have called the police!" Jackie yelled at the woman who didn't have the eyes or ears for the battered spirit. "If you had a little decency to cooperate with them, I may still be alive! I was giving my heart and soul and all the shit about delivering the best-ever Genie on stage! Winning a major part in *Aladdin* was my dream come true and... and...."

Jackie was crying and screaming and practically glowing in blue. A powerful gust of wind blew as she sparkled like a thunderbolt, and we flinched, but the saddest part was whatever Jackie said or did, Paloma never noticed the ghost.

"Why didn't you call the police?" I demanded when the wind weakened. "You should have shown a little decency! If you had informed the police, Jackie, the fourth victim and your husband's coworker, would be alive today! Shame on—"

As I ranted, Rick held me from behind, tightly in his arms. "Mandy," he whispered into my ear. "I can imagine how you feel about everything, but we won't learn anything about Jackie's murder by chastising her. So instead, let's have her talk." When he brushed my face, the tips of his fingers were wet, and I realized I was crying.

Rick looked at Paloma. "We happen to be friends of the last victim, Jackson Frederick Orchard, and my partner here is especially close to Jackie. Playing the part of Genie in *Aladdin* on Broadway was her dream, and it was going to come true if only Jackie was alive."

Paloma gasped, "I… I don't know how to make an apology." But her remorse was palpable.

As I calmed down, Rick loosened his embrace around my shoulders. "Can you tell us your reason for not calling the police?"

Paloma took a deep breath and opened her mouth. "I should have notified the police… but I couldn't. I was being a self-centered idiot. Now I believe I should have done the right thing. I should have alerted the police and prevented further killing. Then again, I couldn't do that. I could have just left him behind, but what about Annette? He was her father, and once Ryan was convicted of not just a murder but serial murders, that was going to stigmatize my child as a lunatic serial killer's daughter. I could and should have turned him in to the police, but I didn't… wasting my time by delaying one day, and then another, completely preoccupied about my future with my daughter—the child of a monster. I'm… I'm so sorry." She clasped her hands together like she was praying.

Jackie bit her lower lip. I raised my hand, reaching for her, though we both knew we couldn't touch each other. I wanted her to know that I supported her. Jackie moved her hand as if she were wrapping her fingers around mine.

"Torn between my selfishness and what little conscience I had left, I kept procrastinating, and perhaps God decided to punish me by taking my daughter away from me. My husband had a car wreck, not only killing himself but her as well. Annette… she did nothing to deserve that." Tears trickled down Paloma's face. "I wished I was dead… to be with my baby girl… but I didn't even have the courage to kill myself."

Rick crossed his arms. "I see. And I'm presuming that the strings of tragedy led you to Aurora Westwood."

Paloma nodded. "Yes. I was practically going insane, and I had no idea how to deal with my loss and devastation. So I read every book I could lay my hands on about spirituality, religion, and everything… magic, even. These books didn't solve my problem, and it was the same thing as doing nothing, but I was desperate to reassure myself by at least trying to do something, anything. And after what seemed like an eternity, I had a chance to have a counseling session with Madame Aurora Westwood. So, I confessed everything."

My eyes widened. If I recalled it right, a counseling by Aurora Westwood cost a small fortune. Actually, there was a time when I considered seeking spiritual guidance from her. I knew it was ridiculous, considering I hated her guts after meeting with the evil witch. Then again, back then, I was a wreck following my expulsion from med school and the

Grim Reaper moniker and everything. It was solely a financial reason that kept me from seeking help from her.

"And what was Aurora's reaction?" Rick's voice brought me back to the present.

"She told me it was no use reporting to the police about my dead husband. She also told me to stop tormenting myself as I'd suffered enough, and... I accepted her advice with gratitude. Back then, I felt like I was pardoned and salvaged...."

"I see. Aurora rocked at acquiring loyal followers or what?" Rick muttered.

Paloma went on. "After the counseling, I forgot about my husband and I started working for Madame Westwood. Of course, there were times that I couldn't stop thinking about Annette, but I tried to forget about my daughter as well, despite knowing it was impossible." She gave a weak smile.

"When and why did you decide to abduct Julie?" Rick asked calmly.

"When I met Julie for the first time in the corridor of Lincoln Center, Madame Westwood said my daughter would be around her age if Annette were alive... and something snapped in me. I had been suppressing my feelings about my daughter for all those years, but at that moment, I couldn't pretend that I'd left my past behind anymore. I knew her name, and I could easily find her on Instagram, and I found the photos had location information, and I presumed one of them to be a private school in the Upper East Side. So I rented a car and followed her from school."

"I see. I'll tell her parents to close all of her social media accounts and stay away from them." Rick frowned.

"When I approached Julie and her guardian, they somehow became absentminded, and Julie voluntarily hopped into my car… and I had a false idea that she wanted to be my child. I now know how stupid and egotistical that sounds, but at that time, raising her as my daughter seemed like my destiny."

"So, Aurora was helping you in the process of kidnapping, wasn't she?" I said.

"No! Not at all." Paloma shook her head violently. "Everything was plotted and committed on my own, and Madame Aurora shouldn't know anything about my crime… I believe. But when Ms. Meyer visited her residence today, Madame looked at me and said, 'Ooh la la, we're having trouble,' so maybe she knew everything. As you probably know, she sees through everything."

I fought the urge to roll my eyes. Saying Aurora Westwood knew everything sounded like an understatement. She had gone so far as to prepare Tyler McGaw as a witness to lead me to her mansion. In addition, the evil witch could have done some dirty trick to make Julie and her guardian absentminded. Oh, don't forget about the surveillance cameras that conveniently stopped functioning during the crucial moments of the kidnapping. On top of all that, Aurora had practically manipulated Paloma into kidnapping Julie.

Paloma's lips quivered. "When I heard Madame's words, I realized that I'd committed a horrible mistake—a mistake that could cost Madame Westwood's dignity. I couldn't just ruin her like that after all those years of providing me with moral support and a meaning in life. And... I felt I had to end my life. At the same time, it occurred to me that I'd be able to reunite with Annette by ending my life in this world. I don't remember how I came here, but the next thing I knew, I was being restrained by the officers. I apologize for all the trouble. And, like I said, I'm better off dead because I deserve death. Don't you think so?"

Paloma lifted the corners of her lips; it looked as if she were trying to force herself to put on a smile, or something was jamming the signal transduction between her brain and facial muscles. Still, I'd never seen such a sad face before.

Jackie took a deep breath and looked over at the sky. "I'm still having a hard time saying, 'Apology accepted,' but... she doesn't have to die. Her death won't revive me or anything." She turned to me. "Mandy, can you tell her not to kill herself?"

"Okay." I nodded, then said to Paloma, "You have to live."

"But—"

"Ms. Seymour," Rick interjected, "as a member of law enforcement, I don't encourage you to harbor criminals, but I can understand the situation you were in. You have to live and apologize to Julie and her parents."

Paloma was silent for a while. After what seemed like an eternity, she said, "May I kill myself after making my apologies to them? I'm so tired of dealing with my feelings."

"No." Rick shook his head. "I don't care about your feelings, but if you die now, your death will leave a permanent scar on Julie's heart. If you sincerely regret what you've done, you have to face the trial and accept whatever penalty is presented for compensation. I'm asking you not as a law enforcement officer but as a friend of Julie and her parents."

"I see... I'm not even allowed to die," she mumbled cheerlessly.

"Mandy, look there," Jackie said, pointing toward Paloma's lower body.

I followed her finger, and then I gasped. "Oh...."

"What?" Rick looked at me with an arched eyebrow.

"Well...." I hesitated for some seconds, but then I turned to Paloma. "Perhaps you might have heard from Aurora, but sometimes I can see dead people."

"Oh, yes." She nodded. "I've heard about your ability from Madame Westwood. She wasn't happy when you solved a murder case before she arrived at the scene."

For the first time, I was glad about Paloma's background working for Aurora Westwood. Under normal circumstances, people would point at me and whisper something in line with "She's sick in the head, poor thing," but she was familiar with the spiritual world.

Paloma was frowning, her expression a

mixture of anxiety and skepticism.

"I see a little girl standing by your side. She's about this tall." I moved my hand to indicate the ghost's height. "And she has the most beautiful hazel eyes and curly blonde hair around her heart-shaped, fair-skinned face with some lovely freckles."

The ghost of a little girl waved her hand at me, and I waved back. When Brian exorcised the hateful ghosts from Paloma's body, I didn't see that girl. Perhaps she sensed my surprise, as she said, "I was sad because I couldn't come near Mommy when she was surrounded by mean people."

I conveyed the girl's words to Paloma, and her jaw dropped, her mouth forming an O. "E-excuse me... but... are you...? But...." Her lips quivered as if she was desperate to enunciate her lost daughter's name.

"She says she's so worried about her mommy and can't leave you. You know what? She's been with you the whole time."

"Annette... she's been with me the... whole time?" Paloma's eyes welled up with tears.

"Yes." I nodded. "You have to stop grieving and start living your own life so that she can stop worrying about you and go to a better place."

"I... have to... live my... own life?"

"Annette is holding your right hand. Do you feel anything?" I asked.

"I-I feel... warm." Paloma put her trembling left hand over the right, as if she were attempting to hold Annette's little hands clasping hers. Annette smiled contentedly at her mother.

"I feel so warm." Fat tears fell from Paloma's eyes, wetting her hands. "I feel so warm." She repeated the phrase over and over.

Five minutes later, the FBI agents arrived and escorted her out of the hospital. As we followed them, Rick's phone dinged.

"Any good news?" I asked him as he glanced at the screen.

"Yup. Jules was found unharmed and the first thing she was heard saying was, 'I'd like some ice cream, please.' She's fine," he said, snorting.

I nodded, grinning like an idiot. "Wow, I'm so glad she's doing fine. Hey, Jackie. Thank you so much for your help. You know what? You've practically saved—" I faltered midsentence. I raised my voice. "Jackie? Where are you?"

"What? Is something wrong?" Rick asked as panic seeped into my voice.

"It's Jackie. She's not answering me," I said, and then I clapped my hands. "Jackie? Where are you? I know you're listening in from somewhere. Let's stop playing hide and seek!"

Silence.

"Hey, Jackie! That's not even funny! Come on, Jackie!" I tried to laugh it off as a prank, but I knew I was just fooling myself.

"Is she answering you?" Rick touched my arm.

"No." I shook my head.

"Jackie, stop hiding and come out." Even when Rick barked his command at her, the ghost of a drag queen didn't answer, much less pop up from out of nowhere like she always did.

"I can't believe this. She's been with me for over a year, and she was around until just a few minutes ago," I muttered, feeling terribly light-headed and wobbly. "It's like she's—" I didn't get to finish my sentence.

Suddenly, my sight blacked out and all of my sensory perceptions were shut down. Passing out, I realized Jackie had left for a better place… without even saying goodbye.

CHAPTER 11

On Saturday of the next week, I was visiting the sidewalk on Upper East Side.

While I had been passed out at the hospital where Paloma Seymour was arrested and Jackie disappeared, I had a weird dream in which someone kept telling me about a boy called Matt Weisberger.

According to the voice, Matt was Tyler's BFF, and he was the person who would help Tyler's departure for a better place. The voice told me to find Matt and bring him to the ghost of Tyler. When I woke up, I attempted to do exactly what I was told, except my plan stayed unexecuted for a week, partly because I had to be hospitalized overnight, and after being discharged, I started running a fever.

The following three days after returning to Rick's condo on the Fifth Avenue, I spent most of the time in bed, wondering if the voice was Jackie's. After a thorough examination, I was given a clean bill of health and the doctor said I was just having an acute reaction to stress and fatigue. Still, Rick was practically frantic over my condition. I'd never seen him so anxious, and for the first time, I learned he could actually cook.

Under normal circumstances, I would have been flattered to the point of doing a happy dance behind his back, but…. Okay, so, you don't see him making pancakes in the kitchen very often, and to be honest, his pancakes tasted way more delicious than what I usually made. Typically, yummy food tended to help lift my mood even in my darkest moments, but this time, nothing worked.

I was depressed—no, depressed was an understatement. I was devastated over Jackie's departure.

Since losing her on the rooftop of the hospital, I hadn't seen or heard from the ghost of a drag queen, and I missed her. When I was in med school, patients died on a regular basis. Each death used to be just a routine, and most of the time, I'd barely known the patients in the first place. Seeing the people departing out of life at the hospital was a synonym for mumbling condolences sympathetically and displaying a solemn face. I didn't really miss those passing patients because I didn't know them so well in the first place.

But this time, things were different. I missed her. I was beyond shocked. Unlike people dying in the hospital, Jackie had no sign of death—okay, so she'd been dead since we met, but she was always cheerful and lively and had a happy-go-lucky attitude. To think back, she was noisy, nosy, annoying, and she obviously found pleasure in driving me crazy sometimes, but… she had been an important part of my life.

On top of all that, I didn't see her disappearance coming. She was gone without even a goodbye, and I wasn't sure if she'd departed to a better place on her own will or if someone had forcibly removed her from this world. At first, I suspected Aurora Westwood might have exorcised

Jackie out of spite for me, but that scenario didn't sound very likely.

According to the news, Aurora was in cardiac arrest when she was rushed to the hospital. The doctors at Presbyterian had managed to resuscitate her. She was on life support for three days, and when she woke up, she had no memory of her life as Aurora Westwood, the most celebrated TV psychic in the world.

I was skeptical about the accuracy of the news at first, and so was Brian, who regarded Aurora as a synonym for a demon. In an attempt to see what was going on, he paid a visit to her at the hospital as a concerned friend. According to him, the old woman was out of the ICU, but her condition seemed tragically bad—as in generalized amnesia or someone at an advanced stage of Alzheimer's disease—and she didn't respond to him even when her name was called. The possibility of Aurora faking her ailment crossed his mind, but he couldn't come up with any good reasons for her to fake her mental disease, especially considering that she had over a dozen TV shows scheduled, including her flagship show *Breaking Dawn with Aurora Westwood*.

Anyway, Aurora's office had recently made an announcement of retirement due to her ill health.

Meanwhile, I had been suffering from a series of sobbing attacks more often than I was comfortable. Rick called my mom, who dropped by his condo bringing dinner, desserts, and the merry women of the Meyers that included Nana, my younger sister Alicia, and her daughters Emma and Minty.

My super-energetic, overly nosy folks turned out to be a great distraction, especially when Nana casually asked, "Mandy, are you pregnant?" I shook my head immediately—after all, they ran all sorts of tests, including pregnancy testing—but Rick choked on a big bite of pot roast.

"Are you sure?" Nana wasn't convinced. "We Meyers tend to be extra-emotional during the early phase of pregnancy."

"I know!" Alicia chimed in. She turned to Rick. "No worries. Dad happens to be a gentle-hearted nice guy. He didn't try to shoot Tony when I conceived Emma."

Her comments made Rick cough harder, but when he recovered, he held my hand, muttering, "I'm glad I don't have to worry about getting shot by your dad." Which prompted Mom to secretly pump her fists under the table, and brought a long-lost smile on my face.

"So, is the boy ghost over there the Tyler boy you were talking about?" Brian's question brought me back to the present as he pointed at the brownstone. The tone of his voice was perky. Following Aurora's retirement, he got several gigs in show biz, and he openly appreciated me for nixing the most powerful psychic from the TV industry. Though I didn't want to accept Brian's thanks, because that would mean admitting that I'd actually harmed Aurora, Rick emphasized my favor for Brian so that he would do some free gigs for us without complaining. Perhaps Rick was right because Brian came to speak to Tyler, and for the first time, the exorcist didn't make a fuss about working a freebie.

"Yes." I nodded. Just like the time when I was desperately looking for witnesses for Julie's kidnapping, Tyler was standing in front of a macaroon shop. He was looking bored, but unlike the first time I saw him, he wasn't sleeping anymore. As I recognized his shape clearly, I realized I could still see ghosts. When I stopped seeing Jackie, I suspected I might have lost my ability to see and communicate with dead people, but that didn't seem to be the case.

"That building... is he still there?" Matt Weisberger gasped. "Um... I had a little suspicion about you being a hoax, if I may say so."

"Of course Tyler's there, and that's why you volunteered to come with us. You want to talk to your buddy, right?" Rick patted the high school sophomore on the back.

"Y-yes... but can you see him, too? I can't see Tyler, and it looks like I'm the only one who can't find him," Matt said hesitantly. When we contacted him a few days ago, he reacted as if he had been awaiting someone from law enforcement to come get him. Brian did the talking as he was known as an exorcist, and when he mentioned Tyler's ghost, Matt mumbled his confession and his will to accept any punishment for Tyler's death. So, as a *punishment*, Rick told him to come to the building where Tyler died so Brian could convey the message to him from Tyler.

Rick shrugged. "Don't worry. You're not alone here. I can't see or talk to dead people either."

"Mandy, perhaps it's better if you talked to

him because he knows you," Brian suggested.

"I agree with you." I nodded and did a little finger wave at the ghost of Tyler McGraw.

"Hi, Tyler. How are you?"

The boy ghost looked at me and smiled. "Oh, you're the person who came here with Jackie. How is she doing? I haven't seen her in forever."

"Um… she's busy," I mumbled. I wasn't ready to admit Jackie was gone. Resisting the urge to sob, I forced a smile on my face. "By the way, we found the kidnapped girl, and she's fine and unharmed. Thank you so much!"

The boy ghost's eyes widened as they shifted to something behind me. "Matt?" Tyler turned to me. "You brought him to me." When he spotted Brian, he frowned. "He's an exorcist, isn't he?"

"Yes. This is Brian Powers, and like you said, he's an exorcist, but don't worry. I didn't bring him to exorcise you," I said. "I've been feeling a tad bit frail lately, and I wasn't sure if I could communicate with you at all. So I brought Brian to make sure someone could relay your words to Matt."

"Hello, Tyler." Brian raised his hand. "Mandy told me the reason you're still stuck here."

"Is he really here?" Matt asked, squinting as if he was hoping to see his deceased friend by doing so.

"Yes, he's right here in front of you." I indicated Tyler with the palm of my hand.

"Hey, Matt. How're you doing?" Tyler waved at Matt, who didn't respond. "Okay, I know you can't hear or see me, but I had to try."

I relayed his words to Matt, and his lips

started to quiver. "Look, Tyler, I'm so sorry for what I've done and… I don't know how to make amends. I shouldn't have left you dying. I should have tried something to help you."

"Don't be sorry. I screwed up when I tried to hold on to the railing. You didn't push me or anything, and it was a pure accident peppered with bad luck that I fell and died. Besides, my death happened instantly, and I was already dead when you were leaving. There was nothing you could do, so stop beating yourself up for my death. I want you to forget about me and live your life. I want you to play football again," Tyler said firmly, looking into Matt's eyes. Tyler took a step toward Matt and tried to hug his friend. Of course, his arms went through Matt's upper body, but Matt shuddered as if he'd felt something.

"Still, I'm sorry," Matt started, but then he looked at Brian and then at me. "What? Did you do anything to me? Why do I feel so… warm and relaxed?"

"That's because Tyler's hugging you," Brian told Matt. "He wants you to quit blaming yourself and start living your life again. Also, he says his death was an accident and you didn't do anything. He's practically begging you to stop blaming yourself because his death happened immediately."

"Also, he wants you to play football again," I added.

"That's… unbelievable," Matt muttered almost to himself. "But somehow, I'm feeling as if Tyler's standing by my side. Maybe I'm going insane."

"No, you're not crazy." Brian shook his head. "He's by your side."

"Yup, and to be honest, I have a hunch you and Susan will make a cute couple," Tyler chimed in, patting his friend's back.

When I told him about Tyler's opinion, Matt displayed an expression resembling a smile. "Seriously? Susan and me?" His jaw, which was previously clenched tightly, loosened up a little.

"Yup, I'm serious." Tyler was smiling from ear to ear.

I noticed the outline of the boy ghost blurring, so I looked at Brian. "Doesn't he look…?"

"Yeah." The exorcist nodded. "He's fading, meaning Tyler's leaving for a better place. Looks like I wasn't that needed in the first place. Perhaps all Tyler wanted was someone sending his message to Matt."

"Still, you've done a good job persuading Matt to come here," Rick said.

"I know," Brian bragged.

The ghost of Tyler McGraw turned to us. "Thank you, guys, for letting me speak with Matt. Now it's time to go, I guess." He winked at us, waving and walking up to the sky as if he were taking the stairway to heaven.

Brian and I waved back at him. Matt and Rick did the same a moment later.

"Thank you, guys. Life's beautiful. Enjoy!" Tyler gave a thumbs-up and left.

As he disappeared, I felt a warm breeze

caressing my face.

Spring was just around the corner. Tyler was gone, and so was Jackie.

"Is he... gone?" Matt asked, looking over the blue sky.

"Yes," Brian said. "He told you that life is beautiful and to enjoy yours."

Matt lowered his gaze and nodded. "I'll try. Thank you, all of you. I don't know how to put it, but it felt like Tyler was really talking to me. I know I'm sounding crazy, but I guess I caught some of Tyler's words with my own ears and... it's...." He fumbled with his words.

"Amazing?" Rick asked.

"Yes." Matt nodded, and then his face turned solemn. "So what's next for me? Are you going to arrest me or something?"

"That's a good question." Rick crossed his arms. "So, technically, you should have called an ambulance or something, but the coroner's report agrees with Tyler's ghost that his death happened immediately and no life-saving efforts could have helped him. So why don't you accept Tyler's words and live *your* life?"

Matt's ears turned red and his face was contorted like he was trying his best not to cry. "Thank you... for everything. I'll live a life that Tyler would be proud of," he said, sniffling.

"Atta boy." Rick smacked the young boy's back. "Now you can quit crying and go home."

Matt left, mumbling, "It's just a stupid allergy," still sniffling.

When Matt turned the corner and went out of our sight, Rick turned to me. "You're quiet, Mandy. Are you all right?" Cupping my face in his hands, his mesmerizing green eyes were fizzling with concerns.

"I'm good. Peachy. Thanks!" I forced a smile and tried my best to speak like everything was fine, but my voice was quivering.

An emotion that was unreadable to me crossed his face, and he said, "Let's go to Pier 26. Brian, come with us. Four eyes are better than two."

* * *

Thirty minutes later, we were standing in the greenway at Pier 26, where I bumped into Jackie for the first time.

Just like the time Jackie and I found each other, the place was filled with joy and happiness. It was a sunny day, and I watched people running, playing basketball, walking dogs, and kayaking in the Hudson.

"Where did you meet Jackie for the first time?" Brian asked me.

"Right there—she came out from there." I pointed at the basketball court.

"I see." Brian squinted.

"Do you see any signs of her?" Rick asked.

"No." Brian shook his head. "It looks like Jackie's left this world. She's practically unmissable. Imagine a drag queen in a skintight outfit in neon pink and green."

"Don't forget the 'FESTIVE' necklace," I

chimed in, chuckling. "Can you imagine my surprise when I saw her for the first time? She was in really bad shape with messy hair and a bloody torso with part of her intestine sticking out of the wound. When I saw her tear-streaked face and heard her shrieking for help, I thought I'd just bumped into an assault victim and… I was mad. Just like now, this place was packed with fun-loving people, but nobody reached out to help her, and they seemed to be looking the other way. When I noticed I was the only person here who could see her, I thought—no, I wished that I was being pranked."

"I know the feeling," Brian muttered.

Rick reached for my shoulders, pulling me close to him. "You weren't thrilled to know her at first. Remember the time you bought an antighost charm from a street vendor?"

"Yeah, I remember. That charm turned out to be totally bogus. When I pointed the charm at Jackie, saying, 'Take it!' she was like, 'Huh?'" I giggled. "I felt like I was being stalked by a weird ghost, and I was so very desperate to get rid of her… but now… now that she's gone, I miss her. It feels like a part of me—a part that's crucial to making me who I am—is missing… and I really, *really* wanted to share the information about her killer, such as the tracksuit and the knife with Jackie's blood were found in Paloma's apartment… and…."

I didn't get to finish my sentence because I was openly sobbing.

"Mandy, look at me." Rick held me by the shoulders, his green eyes staring directly into mine. "I can imagine you're upset over Jackie's disappearance, but considering your bond with her, I don't think she'd just ditch you. I'm sure Jackie's afterlife was happier after knowing you, so stop crying and smile. I'm begging you. You'd be happy if Jackie's left for a better place, where she doesn't feel the pain or agony anymore, wouldn't you?"

He had a point, but the word "ditch" pulled my grief trigger and I wailed. "Nothing stays the same. Things change and people leave. Even my guardian angel has left!"

At that point, I wasn't really sure what I was grieving in the first place, but I was in a zone—a zone for bawling like a drunken idiot. I caught Brian flinching as if he wished he were anywhere but around me, but I didn't care. "I'm not sure how long I'll be able to keep my job with the FBI… as you'll be leaving the feds someday and once you're out they don't need me anymore… and…." As I went on, my devastated-o-meter ran off the chart. I was utterly, totally heartbroken.

"Stop it!" Rick snapped, pulling me closer and holding my shoulders tightly. "Many things constantly change, but some things will stay, as in forever. For example, I'm here with you, and I intend to stick with you. I love you, and I'll stay with you for better or worse, for richer or poorer, and in sickness and health—"

"As long as you both shall live."

When Brian chimed in, I raised my tear-streaked, most likely blotchy face, to look at the exorcist practically grinning like Garfield who'd just found a large dish of lasagna hidden in the fridge. "Hey, Rowling, have you noticed that you just made a marriage proposal?"

"Wha—?" Rick opened his mouth, then closed it shut. He looked at me and then at Brian, his usually flawless skin turning slightly pink.

Then I heard the familiar husky yet perky voice shrieking in my ear. "Oh my God! Did I just hear the words of a marriage proposal? What did I miss? What happened while I was away? Come on, Mandy, you have to share all the juicy details with me!"

"Jackie, you don't need to scream! I'm not deaf!" I snapped. After a pause, I came to my senses. "Did I just say Jackie?" I looked at Rick and then at Brian. I blinked. Then I kept blinking about a dozen times. In front of me, a familiar face was bouncing—except Jackie was sporting a goatee and a blue Genie costume that time.

"Hi there, Mandy. Did you miss me?" As she waved at me, I caught a glimpse of her 'FESTIVE' necklace gleaming at her neckline—with more glitter and beauty than ever.

"Where have you been?" I narrowed my eyes. "How could you ghost away like that? You could have said a goodbye, at least!"

"Because I *am* a ghost?" she said, sounding more like a question than a statement, prompting me to wish I could shake the ghost until her teeth fell out. "Ow, sorry about that. I wasn't planning on that sudden disappearance, but the moment I had a sense of closure, I got detained by a couple of guys in black suits à la *Men in Black*. You know what? Heaven has this agency that is equivalent to our Customs and Border Control, and the men in black happened to be the agents from there. I was detained for overstaying my visa, and I had to be deported until my visa was renewed. I was totally shocked to learn that I was an illegal alien. Who knew dead people need a visa?"

My jaw dropped. A part of me wished I could witness the men in black from Heaven, and a part of me was relieved not to see the agents from Heaven, for they might have tried to manipulate my memory. And if they did, I might have forgotten about Rick as well... such as he's my boss and live-in boyfriend, and I love him so much. *Zap!* and just like that....

"Anyway, now that my visa's renewed and all the issues with my immigration status have been cleared, I'm back. Though I have to always keep my visa up-to-date to avoid overstaying." Jackie bounced and looked into my face. "Hey, Mandy, look at your red nose and puffy eyes! You been crying over me or what?"

"It's an allergy," I lied. "By the way, what happened to your wardrobe?"

"Oh this?" The ghost proudly struck a pose. "I always wanted to show you what an awesome Genie I would have made. What do you think? Impressed?"

"Yes, I'm... overwhelmed," I admitted.

"Woohoo!" Hooting, she flipped and sang the first chorus of "Friend Like Me" from *Aladdin*.

I clapped my hands in appraisal and Brian joined. "Bravo!" Rick said as I told him about Jackie's performance.

"Thank you! I love you all!" Jackie blew a kiss at us, and then with a snap of her finger, she changed into her usual drag queen getup in neon colors. That time, the wound on her side was gone and her intestines weren't visible anymore.

"Jackie, what's happened to your injury? It's... healed!" I exclaimed.

"Oh yes. The wound had already healed nicely when I reached the detention center. They said that's because of having closure with my past. By the way, speaking of love, can I be your maid of honor at your wedding with Rick?"

I opened my mouth to say something, but I didn't know what to say, so I closed it shut. "Jackie... I mean...."

"What did she say?" Rick asked me.

"Jackie says she wants to be the maid of honor for Mandy's wedding," Brian told Rick. "If you want to be the groom at her wedding, I suggest you pop the question before she gets hitched to someone else."

Rick hit his forehead with the base of his palm, muttering, "Oh, crap... so, I've bought the ring, but I'm not carrying it today. I wasn't expecting this."

"What? Was that your reason for the procrastination?" Brian snorted and turned to me. "Mandy, give me your ring." I nodded and handed him the one Rick gave me, and Brian handed it to Rick. "There you go, pal. You can give her the one with a rock later."

Rick took a deep breath. "Mandy, actually I was going to ask you this particular question with a bigger ring, and at a pretty resort or something, at least at a nice restaurant, but everything I told you previously is what I truly feel about you. I love you, and I want to get older with you." Then he dropped on one knee and offered his hand to me. "Amanda Vivian Meyer, will you marry me?"

My heart stopped for a second. Then I opened my mouth. "Y-y-yes! I will... I will!" I said, accepting his hand and feeling the ring being slipped back onto my ring finger. I was crying again, but that time, I was deliriously happy. "Yes, Jackie. You can be my maid of honor."

"Congratulations!" Brian applauded. "By the way, I recommend hiring me for your wedding service, okay? I'm a priest, and I have all the qualifications for conducting a wedding ceremony."

"Oh my God! Oh my God!" Jackie shrieked. "What am I going to wear?"

New Yorkers are notorious for being blasé to others but that time, passersby applauded and congratulated us. But I didn't get to answer them with a smile or a wave of my hands. By the time what had just happened sank in my mind, I was holding on to Rick and kissing him passionately.

EPILOGUE

"Oh, Jules, you must have been so scared!" Loretta Fender, one of her classmates from school, exclaimed.

"Not really." Julie shrugged. About two weeks following her kidnapping, her parents decided to throw a celebration party. "I don't remember much of anything. It was like having a long, dreamless sleep… and the next thing I knew, I was in a familiar place. I looked around and saw the oh-so-stylish furniture and the gold drapes. I recognized the place as a classic room at the Plaza, and I remembered I wanted to have some ice cream."

"Oh, you're so very brave! I'm proud of you!" Eva Margory, another classmate, hugged Julie.

"Why, thank you!" Julie cooed, but her heart wasn't feeling the excitement she should have at the party to celebrate her survival from a dreadful—which wasn't her exact word, more like her parents'—kidnapping.

"Isn't it like… extraordinary?" Eva went on.

Julie wasn't sure what was so extraordinary, but she didn't bother asking. Eva had this nasty habit of exaggerating everything so Julie went into autopilot mode, nodding and smiling like she was really enjoying the conversation. Instead, she was recalling the series of events at the time of her rescue.

When she found herself alone in the hotel room, Julie was slightly surprised, for she was in an extra-frilly pink dress like a costume a beauty pageant contestant would wear, but then her mind wandered off about her craving for ice cream. When she noticed her parents weren't around, her heart was torn between calling room service for an ice cream or her mom's cell. Before she could decide, the door burst open and a bunch of FBI agents barged in.

Brian Powers was among the agents. While Julie stood frozen in the middle of the hotel room, he approached her, asking, "Are you all right?" When she nodded, Brian told her that she had been kidnapped on the way to her granny's place, but there was no need to worry because now she was being rescued.

Nodding at his explanation, she asked, "Where's Rick?"

"Oh Rick? He's interrogating the culprit who kidnapped you," he said gently. "Jules, you have no idea how worried he's been about you. He and Mandy worked really hard to locate you, and finally, we've found you."

"Oh… really," Julie said, trying to keep the disappointment out of her voice.

Following the incident, Julie kept wondering why Rick didn't come for her. She was so preoccupied with that lingering thought that she couldn't provide an immediate answer to Stan Goldman, her classmate, about the invitation for a Disney World trip.

As she frowned, regurgitating the bitter memory of Rick's no-show, her mom called to her from behind. "Julie, darling. How's the party girl doing?"

"Fabulous, Mom. Thank you!" Since the kidnapping, her parents had been super-protective—too protective for her comfort—and Julie didn't bother turning back, but then she caught the voice she'd been longing to hear so badly.

"Hey, Jules. How are you?"

"I'm feeling wonderful! Thank you so much, Rick… and thank you so very much for finding me." Julie turned, smiling, feeling the bliss of meeting the love of her life, but then her smile froze.

"Actually, Jules, Mandy here is the person who did most of the work in finding your location. So you'll want to thank her," Rick said breezily. His green eyes were gentle, and his face was sporting a dazzling smile, but his arm was entwined with Mandy's. On top of all that, Mandy had a rock on her finger.

"Hi, Julie." Mandy smiled. "You look pretty."

"Hi, Mandy. Thank you so much for helping me." Julie forced a smile. She wasn't all that grateful for Mandy, but she wasn't keen on looking like an ungrateful brat. "By the way, I like your ring." She reached for Mandy's left hand.

"Thanks." Mandy giggled, letting Julie touch the huge diamond. Her face had a happy glow.

"I'm glad you like the ring, Mandy. It didn't come cheap," Rick chimed in. Then he bent his tall frame to meet Julie's eyes. "So, I know you and Mandy have previously met each other, but I'd like to formally introduce my fiancée to you. This is Mandy, the future Mrs. Rowling." He then straightened up and looked at his fiancée hanging on his arm. "Mandy, this is Jules, my BFF."

Julie felt like breaking down and crawling on the floor of the banquet room at the Plaza Athénée, but she was too proud for a temper tantrum. Instead, she looked Rick in the eyes. "Are you sure you love her? As in madly?"

"What? Are you interrogating me?" Rick seemed a little taken aback by Julie's question.

"Darling, it's rude to talk like that to a gentleman," her mother interjected, but Rick brushed her off, saying, "It's okay, Meredith. We're BFFs after all." Then he looked back at Julie without the slightest sign of hesitation. "Yes, I love her, as in madly."

"Oh… really?" Julie turned to Mandy. "What about you, Mandy? Do you really, really love him?"

"Yes." Mandy blushed. "As in really, really, really."

"You hear that?" Rick flashed his perfect set of pearly whites at Meredith. "I should have recorded that," prompting Mandy to lightly smack his arm.

"Oh," Julie muttered, pouting. Then she said to Mandy, "In that case, you can call me Jules. Considering your relationship with Rick and that you've helped me, now I can regard you as my special friend."

"Why thank you!" Mandy's face lit up. "I'm so happy!"

"Me, too." Julie forced a smile while catching her mom rolling her eyes.

"Hey, Jules, how're you doing?" Stan

Goldman spoke to her as if on cue.

"Hi, Stan. I'm fab!" Julie answered. "By the way, about the trip to Disney World, can I join you?"

"Of course." Stan's mouth quirked up into a smile. Then he turned to Julie's mom. "Dr. Grey, may I invite you and Jules to our family vacation home in Orlando in the coming summer? If schedule allows, I invite the other Dr. Grey—I mean, Jules's dad—as well. What do you think about this plan?"

"That sounds wonderful." Meredith smiled. "I'll talk to your mom and dad, okay?"

"Of course." Stan nodded.

Julie noticed she wasn't upset anymore, even when she saw Rick kissing Mandy.

Acknowledgement

Dear readers,

First of all, thank you so much for reading this book. And for all of you who've read through the Paranormal in Manhattan Mystery series, thank you so much for your continuing support.

When I released my previous book, *Wicked of the Christmas Past*, I heard from many readers, asking if that was the final book of this series—and the answer is no.

I decided to leave a note about the status of this series. This book isn't the final one either. I'd really like to keep up with what's going to happen to Mandy, Rick, Jackie, and the rest of the gang.

In closing, thank you again. Without your support, I'd never have had a chance to see Book 5 of the Paranormal in Manhattan Mystery, and Mandy, Rick, and Jackie urge me to relay their deepest appreciation to you all.

XOXO,
Lotta Smith

About the author

Hi! My name is Lotta Smith. I'm the author of Paranormal in Manhattan Mysteries and Kelly Kinki Mysteries. I love everything comedy, from novels, TVs, to movies. In my teenage days, I was addicted to mysteries that involves amateur sleuth duo of a hot male professor and a quirky female student—with a light touch of romance sprinkled on top. So I went to medical school, partly because I wanted to see *real* dead bodies, and mostly because I was determined to meet sexy professors (specializing forensic pathology, perhaps) and go a-sleuthin'.

I got to see dead bodies and learn about the danger of petting zoos (sometimes, kids have their lips bitten off by…say, a pony!) but unfortunately, sexy professors were absolutely nonexistent. Recently, I realized that I'm a hopeless *un*romantic.

I'm hard at work writing new books.

To hear about new books and discounted book sales, please sign up for my newsletter at: **http://eepurl.com/bOSLYj**

And follow me on **Amazon:** http://amzn.to/22h0TSf

Books by Lotta Smith

Paranormal in Manhattan Mysteries:
http://mybook.to/PIMM

Book 1: Wicked for Hire: http://amzn.to/25IHH6X

Sometimes, the opportunity of a lifetime busts your door instead of gently knocking at it...

FREE on Kindle Unlimited!

Medical student Amanda Meyer thought she had her life all planned out until people started dying the moment they touched her. Being cleared of any wrongdoing didn't stop the medical school from expelling her, and it didn't rid her of the unfortunate nickname Grim Reaper.

Luckily, having a rep as the harbinger of death isn't a total resume killer. Rick Rowling, Special Agent for the FBI's Paranormal Cases Division recruits her to work for the Bureau. But the sexy, brilliant, outrageous loose cannon proves to be just as untouchable as the mysterious creature or creatures that may be responsible for the seemingly unsolvable murder that becomes their first case together.

Instead of treating patients, Amanda's life becomes a test of her patience and a wild ride into the wicked paranormal world where her new boss runs the show. Together they face a ghoulish force that could destroy the entire city and a grueling family dinner that could leave Amanda contemplating harakiri.

It's a battle of life and debt [student debt, that is] and saving the world has never been so funny.

Prologue
966 Park Avenue Tower
11:48 AM, November 10…

With a weird moan, her whole body shivering, she collapses onto the sofa.

I think she's lucky that she's already sitting on the sofa as she crumples. If she was standing, she might have cracked her head on the marble floor like Humpty Dumpty—which won't be pretty.

She's lying there, totally motionless. One elbow's stiffly bent at a right angle, as if she's turned into stone as the result of looking Medusa in the eye.

I gasp—fearing she's dead.

Rick Rowling, the head of the FBI's New York Paranormal Division and my boss for the past two days, approaches and touches her neck. Looking totally blasé, he confirms that she's still alive.

I let out a sigh of relief.

On the other hand, Rowling announces that we leave the place because *"It's boring."*

My eyes widen with a total disbelief.

Of course, I disagree with him, but he brushes off my objection, stating that he doesn't care about all the crap of making arrests, prosecuting, and taking cases to trial. Again, he says that it's just a minor issue and he's way too busy for that. "You know what? I have better things to do," Rowling declares, turning on his heels to leave the condo.

"Excuse me, Rick," I call to his back.

"What?" he asks, without turning around.

"We can't just leave," I say. Then it suddenly

occurs to me that offending my boss isn't in my best interest, so I add, "I'm afraid."

"Why not?" He cocks his head. "Mandy, don't be such a killjoy. The NYPD can work on the boring stuff, such as deciphering the social pathology of crimes and so on, because they have time to kill. On the other hand, I have no time to waste."

"Okay, so we don't need to decipher the social pathology of crimes, but we do need to figure out the whereabouts of the human-eating monster, don't we?" I point out.

I'm not joking or exaggerating.

I'm talking about a practically imperishable ghoul which could eat up the entire population of New York State, if not the whole world.

* * *

At precisely 2:13 in the morning, John Sangenis was standing in front of a shabby five-story apartment in Washington Heights. Fortunately, he didn't live there. He was just visiting Ivan Flynn, the insufferable asshole.

Usually, he had better things to do than visiting his worst enemy before the crack of dawn, such as sleeping like a log. Or making love with Ruth, which was even better than sleeping on his own. Ruth MacMahon was his girlfriend, who was unbelievably beautiful, dazzling, and had a truly big heart. Also, it didn't hurt that she was rich. What was more wonderful about her was she appreciated John's talent as an actor. It was a rare trait to come across in society, and it was why she happily provided him both moral and financial support.

If there were any shortcomings about her, it was that she was two-timing him with Ivan.

He thought about her taste in men, or lack thereof, and shrugged.

John wasn't the sharpest knife in the kitchen, so he didn't realize describing Ruth's taste in men as horrible was the same as admitting that he was a total loser.

A cold, wet late-autumn breeze was blowing from the East River. A sprinkle of rain hit him in the face. The metal stairs were slippery, occasionally letting out squeaks and squawks, as if the steel structure itself were threatening to fall into pieces any minute, which made John nervous. The building's elevator hadn't functioned since God knows when, so he had no choice but to climb up the damned stairs. Getting smashed with the lousy staircase like a piece of garbage wasn't high on his to-do list, so he ran up the stairs.

As an actor, he went to the gym to do occasional workouts and training, but that didn't mean he was a big fan of vigorous exercise. On normal days, he would have shied away from walking up the rusty metal stairs of a sad-looking apartment. Actually, he wouldn't have set a foot in this neighborhood unless he was starring in a gangster movie or TV show, hopefully as the lead role. After all, it wasn't the area where any of the characters of *Sex and the City* lived. It almost felt comical that this neighborhood was still included in Manhattan.

While he mentally dissed Washington Heights, he completely forgot about his own social status as one of the least important actors in off-

Broadway theater scenes. He also conveniently forgot the fact that, if it weren't for the tiny apartment in Brooklyn, which he inherited from a late great-aunt, and financial assistance provided by Ruth, he couldn't even keep a roof over his head.

He jumped and let out a girly yelp when a rat the size of an obese Chihuahua ran up the stairs from behind and went ahead of him.

"What kind of miserable excuse of an unknown artist lives here?" he muttered to himself after some cussing—again, completely forgetting the fact he happened to be one of those miserable excuses himself.

As he approached the third floor where Ivan lived, John remembered his last exchange of words over the phone with his enemy, and being annoyed so greatly that he almost felt like his blood flowed backward.

About thirty minutes ago, he received a strange phone call from Ivan.

Getting a phone call from him was a rare event, mostly because the feeling of hate between the two of them was mutual. Both were Ruth's kept men, and both were trying their best to convince her that the other guy wasn't worth her time—or money.

"Hey, John the loser, I've got bad news for you," Ivan declared as soon as John picked up the call. He sounded like he was drunk, but there was something in his voice that made John nervous.

"What are you talking about?"

"I'm calling to deliver a piece of special news to you. Now that I've acquired something to make me the El Greco of the twenty-first century, you're so out of sight to Ruth and out of the picture. She is going to choose me, and she'll dump you like a piece of garbage. Ha! Why don't you curl up in the corner of your tiny apartment and cry like a little girl?" Then the line went dead.

Immediately, John rushed from his apartment and took a cab to Washington Heights. He was determined to confront the SOB and beat him till he cried like a baby.

As soon as he reached apartment 312, he banged on the door.

"Who's there?" Ivan's voice demanded from inside.

"It's John. Open up."

"No way."

"I have something to say to you. Open up!" John banged on the door even louder.

"Stop bothering me. Just leave!"

"No, I won't. I won't 'just leave' until I get to talk to you face-to-face."

"I have nothing to say to you. You have to leave, or else I'll call the cops and have you—"

It seemed Ivan was about to say "arrested," but his words stopped short.

Instead of menacing words, he let out an agonizing moan. It became louder and escalated to a high-pitched shriek.

Then came silence.

"Hey, Ivan, what's going on?" John asked as he switched from banging to knocking on the door.

No reply.

"Come on, Ivan. Open up. You can't fool me!" John yelled at the door, but again, no reply.

"Guess what, Ivan? You're all words and no action. You're just running away from me because I'm stronger than you. Ha!" John yelled at the door and turned on his heels to leave. After taking a couple of steps, he went back to his love opponent's door.

"Loser!" Yelling, he jumped and kicked at the door. He was just trying to make his point, but the worn-out door made of a thin veneer wood panel broke easily.

John lost his balance and fell onto the cold concrete corridor.

"Crap," he groaned.

Lying on the hard, cold floor, John was half expecting Ivan to come out of hiding, yelling at him, but no one came from inside. Instead, a twentyish Asian guy stormed out from next door.

"What is the matter with you?" he demanded.

John mumbled an apology and the guy went back to his room.

Something wasn't right.

He got up and reached for the now-broken door. It was locked, but he could put his hand inside to unlock the door.

Getting inside was a piece of cake.

"Hello?" John said. "Ivan? Um… Sorry about the door."

As he opened it, dim light came into his eyes.

"Ivan…?"

There was no one in the room.

"What the hell…?" he muttered.

It was a tiny, one-bedroom, matchbox-sized apartment. In the living room / dining room / workroom was a 30" x 40" painting sitting on an easel. It was nothing fancy. The whole background was painted in an assortment of dark, boring, and depressing colors. The only part that caught his attention was the large blank area in the canvas. It looked as if whatever was portrayed had run out of the canvas and vanished.

He advanced closer to the painting.

On the side of the canvas, the title *G.H.O.U.L.* was written in pencil.

Glancing down, John gasped as he spotted an assortment of men's clothes, including underwear, heaped on the floor, as if someone stripped off those garments and left.

Or whoever had those garments on had disappeared like smoke.

"Hey, Ivan?" Not grasping the situation, John searched the apartment for his rival, but he couldn't find any signs of him.

John glared at the heap of clothes in front of the canvas for a while. Then, out of the blue, he kicked the garments. As the shirt, pants, and underwear scattered, something like pebbles of stone rolled over the floor.

"What the…?" John picked up a piece. It looked like a tooth—small, white, and hard, with a metal bolt on the base.

As an actor, he liked to play the role of a tough guy, but in reality, he wasn't. Startled, he dropped the tooth on the floor. When it hit, he caught a glimpse of several other pieces. Each was about the size of a chick pea, yellowish white with dark brown stains.

The moment he realized the stains might be blood, John passed out and dropped on the hard floor.

CHAPTER 1

Green and purple… Seriously? Who had the deciding vote in determining the color schemes of this hideous building? USCIS? Or FBI? I wondered as I stood in front of 26 Federal Plaza in Manhattan, my new workplace.

It was my first day of work at the FBI's New York Field Office, and I wasn't sure if I was happy or unhappy about my new career as an FBI special assistant.

If this were a book, movie, or TV show, I would be a budding FBI special agent or something really badass.

In that case, I would be ready to protect and defend the United States as I fought menacing terrorists or a group of evil aliens trying to invade Earth. In addition, if it were fiction, I would look like Jennifer Lawrence and have a really flashy educational background under my belt, such as having graduated from an Ivy League school at the top of my class. Not to mention I would be driving a Ferrari or a Lamborghini, or a Mercedes at least.

Unfortunately, none of the above characteristics applied. After all, I was talking about my life, and lately, it kind of sucked.

My name is Amanda Meyer. I'm a twenty-five-year-old American with Italian, English, and a little bit of Romanian heritage.

I'm an American woman in my mid-twenties, but that's all I have in common with *The Hunger Games* star. I stand at 5'4", and I'm a size or two—or maybe three—larger than her dress size.

I don't have an Ivy League education under my belt, mostly because Harvard, Yale, Columbia, and all other such schools rejected my application. As for the car, I don't even own one. I used to drive a relatively new Toyota Camry, but I sold it. I was trying my best to convince myself I didn't need to have a car anymore now that I moved back to my parents' home in Queens, New York.

About a month ago, I was a medical student in North Carolina. I was in my third year—busy studying for exams, memorizing all the medical and surgical knowledge, and doing clinical rotations—until I got kicked out of medical school.

Don't get me wrong. I wasn't a bad student.

So I didn't hold high hopes of graduating at the top of my class, or someday becoming a Nobel laureate. Then again, my academic performance wasn't that bad. I was usually at around the top 50-60 percent of the class. At a place where the majority of your classmates have an IQ of 180 and up, even being a mediocre student took lots and lots of hard work.

Anyway, the odds of my finishing medical school and becoming a doctor or getting some cushy job with some pharma/biotech/insurance company were pretty high. Back then, I used to picture myself in the future driving a nice car and vacationing in beautiful resorts.

Generally speaking, doctors are highly regarded in today's society. Sometimes, people talked about the top-notch physicians in comparison with God. On the other hand, I was held in comparison with the Grim Reaper and the Angel of Death. And as a result, I got kicked out of medical school, saying good-bye to my life plan as a doctor.

Oh, did I mention getting kicked out of medical school didn't offset my larger-than-life student loan?

So, there I stood, with no degree under my belt and a huge debt up to my eyeballs. To rub salt in the wound, Justin, my now ex-fiancé, had called off our engagement. We went to the same med school. He was two years my senior and was already in his first year of residency training. Obviously, he had assessed the pros and cons of staying with me and concluded that staying with a woman called the Grim Reaper wasn't likely to boost his value as a surgeon.

As I stood in front of the East German-style building, I felt so depressed, I almost started sobbing.

Look at the bright side, Mandy... I tried to convince myself.

At least I was going to have a job, and their offer wasn't bad. I would be able to make monthly payments on my student loan and make a decent living. Maybe I could even move out of my parents' townhouse in a year or so.

Actually, I wasn't eager to take this job when I received the offer, but Mom and Dad insisted I should. They were not very keen on spending the rest of their lives paying off my student loan.

"Miss, you've been standing here for a long time." Frowning, the guy in a guard's uniform gave me an accusing glare.

"Um... I'm sorry. I got a little bit distracted. I'm supposed to start working here today," I said, but based on his deep frown, I was positive he didn't believe me.

"Oh, I'm running late. I've got to go...." I attempted to walk away, but he grabbed my arm.

"What is the purpose of—?" the guard started interrogating me, but he didn't get to finish his sentence.

"Good morning, Stanley," a male voice boomed from behind us. It was a deep, smooth baritone—clear, calm, and confident. Without turning back to see him, I found myself picturing a tall guy with a certain level of sexiness. He continued, "For your information, you don't want to mess with her. Guess what? So far, she's killed three men just by touching them. In addition, it's her first day working as my assistant. If you convince her to leave without even starting the job, Hernandez will be so pissed."

I had a remote knowledge that the head of the FBI's New York Office was named Hernandez.

"Mr. Rowling!" The guard's response sounded more like a surprise than an acknowledgement.

When he straightened himself, he was no longer grabbing my arm, too busy saluting Mr. Rowling.

"I am awfully sorry for my rude behavior. I didn't know she was your new assistant."

Then, turning to me, he apologized profusely. "I'm awfully sorry, ma'am."

If eyes could speak, his were saying, 'Why didn't you mention you worked for *him*?'

"Okay, so we're all cool," said Mr. Rowling.

I turned back to thank and greet him, but words failed me.

He was tall, athletic, and had broad shoulders. He had flawless fair skin and dark hair styled in a conservatively messy 'do. His mesmerizing green eyes looked almost blue, and his cheekbones were prominent. His nose and jaw were sculpted to perfection.

In a nutshell, he was drop-dead gorgeous.

But that wasn't the only reason I was at a loss for words.

"You are the—" Clenching my teeth and fists, I searched for words.

Though I didn't remember his name, I did recognize him, in an 'I am so going to kill him if I ever lay my eyes on him again' way.

"Yeah, I'm Rick Rowling." He flashed his

perfect set of pearly whites. Obviously, he didn't read my mind. "Hi, Mandy. Nice meeting you again." He extended his right hand toward me.

I took a deep breath. I had no fucking idea why this guy was so familiar with me to call me by the nickname I'd used since kindergarten. Before today, we had met only once for just a couple of hours, and during that short period of time, he killed my future as a doctor.

I took his hand, half wishing he'd drop dead on the spot.

After all, he was the one who convinced the Chapel Hill Police Department and my medical school that I'm the Grim Reaper.

Book 2: W is for Wicked:
http://amzn.to/29s5SLj

Murder investigation is tricky—especially when the deceased threatens to kill you...

FREE on Kindle Unlimited!

Former medical student turned FBI special assistant Amanda Meyer isn't thrilled about her new gig as a ghost whisperer, especially now that she has the spirit of a departed drag queen following her around.

But having a pal on the other side may just come in handy when a billionaire's widow meets her untimely demise and Amanda and her oh so sexy boss, Rick Rowling, head of the Paranormal Cases Division, are called in to find the killer.

With nine scandalous suspects, nine questionable motives, one dead witness and one cryptic clue, the bureau's dynamic duo should be able to solve this case by the numbers, but the victim's restless soul wants revenge while the clock is ticking. What's the girl nicknamed The Grim Reaper to do? M may be for Murder, but W is for Wicked.

PROLOGUE

"There are some men who enter a woman's life and screw it up forever."
—***Janet Evanovich, One for the Money***

My name is Stephanie Plum, and for me, the man who takes pleasure in periodically screwing up my life is Joseph Morelli....

No, that's a downright lie—I mean, I'm kidding—for the most part.

I'm not the world's most famous, most popular, or perhaps, the richest female bounty hunter. As for Joseph Morelli, I haven't even met him, much less got screwed by him. Um... don't misunderstand me, I'm talking conceptually, not physically or carnally.

Okay, so I know it's wrong to impersonate a total stranger, but excuse me, you need to cut me some slack.

My life sucks way worse than Stephanie's. Sometimes, I'm oh-so-desperate to fool myself that I have a life somewhere, anywhere but where I'm stuck.

My name is Amanda Meyer. Most of the time, I'm called Mandy, and that's the acceptable part—I can live with this nickname. Like Stephanie, I work in a law enforcement field, except I'm with the FBI instead of a bonds office in New Jersey. Unlike her, I'm not filthy rich. She's described as constantly struggling for money in her books, but I know she's rich.

Okay, so she goes on about how she's stuck with a dead-end job forecasted as mostly cloudy with chances of raining bullets and dead bodies and exploding vehicles, how she ended up selling her electronics, and how little food she's left at home—but that's just her words. On second thought, it's impossible to stay poor when you're the star of a megahit series. She probably has her millions stashed somewhere, such as a private bank in Switzerland. In my previous life, I was anticipating a decent life for my future, if not being obscenely rich. I was going to become a doctor, but that career option is now gone, baby, gone. Thanks to getting booted out of medical school with no degree and a humongous student loan, I'm deep in debt up to my eyeballs.

And, believe me, there actually are some men who pop into a woman's life from out of nowhere—like some kind of a genie, leprechaun, or ghost—with the sole purpose of messing with it.

By the way, did I mention that I have not just one, but two men, hexing my life?

For starters, there's Rick Rowling. He's the head of Paranormal Cases Division at the FBI's New York City field office. He became my boss by practically butchering my medical career before it even started. Standing at 6'2" with lean, hard muscles in all the right places, he's hot, sexy, and comes with intense green eyes. He happens to be the only heir to the huge, multi-billion, security conglomerate USCAB—United States Cover All Bases—which means he's ridiculously rich. Unfortunately, he also happens to be an outrageous, egotistical smartass who'd kill to generate trouble and mayhem just for the sake of his own pastime.

I'm not exaggerating. During the investigation of our first case, we were close to being eaten by a bunch of unperishable, monstrous creatures. So I'm trying my best to keep a good distance from him, but he tends to pop in to dinners with my folks at my parents' home.

And there's another guy, Jackie, also known as Jackson Frederick Orchard, who was a budding Broadway actor.

It all happened last November when Rowling and I were walking Pier 26 in Tribeca, where I saw something—no, *someone*—who should be absolutely discernible…

"Cool!" Rick Rowling grinned while walking in the same park where we met Jackie the day before.

"I know! It's totally fab!" Jackie agreed contently.

They were acting like a couple of nine-year-old boys admiring a new toy. Except, their focus wasn't on a new Xbox or hoverboard that actually lets you float and fly in the air. Also, technically, the two of them weren't communicating with each other.

Jackie could see and hear Rowling, but things didn't work out the other way around, because Rowling couldn't see or hear Jackie, which meant he couldn't see Jackie's revealing, skintight outfit in neon green and hot pink, the big hair like Shakira, or the snow-white boa headdress. Not that my boss had impaired vision or hearing, though… it's complicated. He couldn't even see the huge necklace spelling 'FESTIVE' hanging from Jackie's neck.

It was sad that Rowling missed so many colorful things in front of his eyes. Still, at the same time, he was lucky, since he didn't see the huge laceration on the side of Jackie's abdomen, or the little portion of intestines peekabooing from the wound. On top of all that, Jackie was acting a little bit too intimate toward Rowling—for example, raining him with kisses, trying to grope his derrière, and so on. Though Jackie's hands always went through Rowling's body instead of actually landing on his private areas, my boss seemed somewhat uncomfortable whenever he was touched on his butt. So, he might have been feeling something….

Anyway, I happened to be the hot topic du jour. To be more precise, my newly discovered ability to interact with Jackie was.

"You know what, Mandy? So far, you've totally nailed it. All the details you mentioned were accurate. You even correctly described the parts yet to be disclosed to the media, which means you're actually communicating with Jackie. Holy crap, you're phenomenal!" Rick Rowling announced enthusiastically. "By utilizing your new skill, our case closure rate's guaranteed to hit a new high."

"Well, I don't know…," I mumbled in uncertainty. I glanced at Jackie, who was standing by my side. "Maybe he's the only dead person I can communicate with, or maybe—" *He might be my imagination, illusion, or hallucination*

"Okay, Mandy. Relax." Rowling reached for my shoulder, but before his hand touched me, Jackie butted in between us.

"So, Mandy, are you ready to find the SOB who stabbed me to death? Now that I have shared all the juicy details about my case with you," Jackie, who turned into a ghost after getting murdered, said expectantly.

Yeah, you heard me right. I said Jackie is a ghost. Actually, he's not one of those common, boring ghosts, because he's a ghost of a drag queen, and he's urging me to help catch his killer.

"Of course, I know you're ready to kick ass, considering you've got this hottie hunk FBI agent as a partner. No offence, but I'd love to team up with him without you between us as a translator, and it'd be way nicer if only I could touch him." The ghost of a drag queen chattered nonstop. "By the way, I told you that I preferred to be referred to as *she*, not *he*. I might be a super actor who can be anybody, but I'm a girl at heart." Jackie had the audacity to make tsk-tsk sounds and correct me.

"Um... sorry about that," I mumbled in apology, thinking, *Seriously? A girl at heart? A diva to the bone sounds way more accurate.*

Meanwhile, Jackie went on. "By the way, Mandy, don't even think about pretending you don't see me. You can try shutting your eyes and covering your ears, but you just can't ditch me like old undergarments infesting your closet. I have waited for three years, for Pete's sake! If you abandon me, I'll haunt you like the devil till you go totally cuckoo yourself."

As he—no, *she*—threatened me, the gut peeking out of the wound seemed to be vibrating, as if it represented his—not his, *her*—anger.

Man, she sounds serious... "Oh, no, Jackie, I've never thought about abandoning you!" I flashed a reassuring smile, but inside I wanted to scream and run away. Deep in my mind, I was skeptical about Jackie—like if she *really* exists—and I wanted to state my skepticism loud and clear. But at the same time, if I was a ghost of a murder victim and someone who can hear my voice treats me like I don't exist, I'd be devastated—as if I got murdered not just once but twice. Also, it wouldn't be pretty if the ghost kept to her promise of haunting me like hell. Gosh, I needed a psychiatrist... or a drink strong enough to knock me down unconscious.

"Good." She nodded.

At this time, I knew the chances of the ghost diva departing to a better place like most dead people were practically nonexistent.

"And think of the cool prospects, Mandy." While I was being threatened by Jackie, Rowling's hand had already gone through Jackie and was patting my shoulder. "We can interview dead politicians and high-profile bureaucrats, make them spill their guts, and put our hands on dirty little secrets of our highest-ranking personnel—such as the President of the United States."

"E-excuse me? We? Did you just say *we*?" I stuttered.

"Hmm, that sounds good," Jackie chimed in. "Grasping the VIP's dirty secrets is always good because you can use them as leverage."

"Yeah, it's awesome!" Rowling beamed. "We can practically control the government by utilizing the intel obtained from dead people. Can it get any better?"

I took a deep breath and looked my boss in the eye. "Excuse me, Rick. You told me you can't see or hear Jackie, right?"

"Yup." His intensely deep green eyes looked straight back at me. "Why do you ask that?"

"Hey, Mandy, is there any chance he's gay?" Jackie interjected, trying without success to pick up a lock of brown hair hanging over Rowling's forehead. Before I answered, she continued. "No, he's not gay. I can tell. I can just tell. Assuming he's a straight guy, shouldn't he be swatting me like a bug when I'm getting a little bit too intimate with him? You're so skeptical, Mandy. He's telling you the truth. There is no way he can see or hear me. I recommend you stop doubting. Joy and happiness will run away from you if you keep on taking a dim view of everything."

She had a point. Considering they weren't channeling with each other, I was stuck not only with Rick Rowling but also with Jackie the ghost, who was as outrageous as Rowling.

"Oh, I found another reason to conclude that he can't see me." Jackie went on. "If he's gay or bi, he should be cooing whenever I touch him, shouldn't he?"

Slapping my forehead, I groaned.

"What's up, Mandy?" Rowling and Jackie said in unison as if they had no clue why I looked so grim.

"Never mind," I said, wishing it were just a weird, wicked dream and not my life, or my career....

* * *

Once being born to this world, every life is destined to die—eventually, sooner or later, and at least once. Everybody knows that, but most people do not expect people close to them to suddenly go cold, motionless, and totally uncommunicative, as in a deathly silence, especially when they had no existing serious health problems.

"Holy smoke!"

When Marcus heard those words in Willow's high-pitched voice, he nervously twitched his impeccably trimmed and manicured eyebrows.

It was the moment he heard the telltale *thud!* He was almost certain that the maid had committed another faux pas—like dropping a heavy object, or falling a few steps down the grand staircase—without seeing it for himself, because he had witnessed Willow flopping more often than he wished to see.

Marcus looked at the clock. It was just a few minutes to 9:00 p.m. He couldn't help wondering why the maid had to make another blunder just minutes before finishing her shift and leaving. He sighed, thinking that Willow wouldn't be happy to help fix whatever mess she had created. But when her next wail came saying, *"Madame... Madame! Are you all right?"* he could no longer sit quietly in his waiting room.

As soon as he burst into the foyer, he demanded, "What is the matter, Willow?"

"Oh... Mr. Marcus, I'm so glad you're here!" the maid said breathlessly, without standing.

"Are you—" Marcus started to ask, but then gasped. "Oh my goodness, Madame Giselle!"

To his horror, it was Giselle Carolynn Axtell McCambridge, the head of the McCambridge family, and his very own employer, who was helplessly lying over the bottom steps of the grand staircase. She was bleeding from her head, and the blood was oozing over the white marble step.

Rushing to her side, Marcus inquired, "Madame Giselle? Madame Giselle! Please wake up."

By his side, Willow shrieked, "Madame Giselle!"

"Come on, Willow! Stop shrieking and give me the phone! Now, go and open the gate to secure the access for the ambulance, and notify Mr. Wilfred and Mrs. Wilma-Diane." As Marcus, the butler of the McCambridge mansion, shushed away the maid, Giselle let out a low groan.

"Madame Giselle! Are you all right? Are you hurting?" As soon as he finished speaking to the 911 operator, he peppered his employer with questions.

"Marcus…" twitching her delicate eyebrows, Giselle whispered in her usual commanding voice. "You don't need to scream at me. I haven't gone deaf." Then she grimaced. "Ow… it's so painful!"

Her voice was strong, and her pale gray eyes were piercing as always, but obviously, she was in pain.

"Madame, the ambulance is on the way. Please relax and rest assured—"

"Ambulance? Did I just hear that I'd be riding an ambulance? How embarrassing!" Touching her head, Giselle frowned. "No McCambridge has ever ridden an ambulance."

"Which means you're the very first McCambridge given the honor," Marcus responded, forcing himself to display some humor and a reassuring smile.

"By the way, Marcus," Giselle said, looking at her now bloodstained fingertips, "you need to call the police as well, because someone pushed me off the stairs."

"Oh, my…" The butler gasped, but soon regained his composure. "Who committed such dreadfulness?"

"Marcus, will you collaborate with the police to catch the culprit?" Giselle reached for the butler.

Taking the mistress's hand, Marcus consoled her. "Madame Giselle, you will soon feel better. The doctors at Beth Israel will make sure you'll be as good as…" He stopped talking when he realized Giselle was writing the letter *W* on his palm in blood—over and over. "Madame Giselle?"

He intended to ask her for the meaning of *W*.

"It is by no means acceptable to push someone off the stairs." Before Marcus spoke, Giselle did, looking the butler straight in his eyes. "Marcus, I recall that you like Jeeves, am I correct?"

"Yes, Madame. You are correct. I'm a huge fan of Jeeves." Even though Marcus was dying to ask more about *W*, he knew his mistress too well to butt in. When Giselle McCambridge had something to say, she had to say it, and there was no room for the butler to change the subject.

"Good. Make sure that this crooked criminal who hurt me gets caught and justice is served. Be my Jeeves."

"I will, Madame Giselle. I will be your Jeeves. By the way, who is *W*?"

"*W* is... I mean... find..." As Giselle started to talk, she grimaced and gasped for air. Her entire body convulsed for a moment. Then she closed her eyes, never to open them again.

Find *W*—these were the last words of Giselle Carolynn Axtell McCambridge.

By the time the family members and the visitors came to see what the commotion was about, Giselle had become unresponsive.

The paramedics arrived and took her to Beth Israel, but even the world's greatest physicians couldn't bring her back to life.

Giselle's death was a total shock to Marcus. Considering her advanced age—seventy-seven, that was, though she stopped counting since hitting fifty—Giselle was extremely healthy, and her death was unexpected. At the same time, Marcus knew that solving the assault, which was upgraded to a murder, of Giselle McCambridge had become the last mission assigned by his employer for the past twenty-five years. By filling the blanks and reading between the lines of his previous conversation with his employer, he knew that *W* was the culprit.

Under normal circumstances, the most straightforward answer would be someone with names starting with W. And considering that there was no burglar at McCambridge mansion at the time of the crime, it was only natural to assume that whoever committed this crime would be someone at the house.

The only problem was everyone at the McCambridge mansion at the time of the crime had at least one W as the initial of their names—including Marcus Warne-Smith himself.

Book 3: Wicked Little Secret: http://amzn.to/2du4JWy

Everyone has secrets--ghosts are no exception...

FREE on Kindle Unlimited!

Finding her body taken over by a ghost with unfinished business while entertaining a tempting (yet dangerous sounding) invitation from Rick Rowling--her boss--has Amanda Meyer, FBI special assistant and resident ghost whisperer for the Paranormal Cases Division, in a tailspin. Her drag-queen-guardian ghost is acting even stranger than usual, a murder victim holds a clue to finding a stolen sculpture, and a parade of well-meaning family members might just set another murder in motion.

What's the girl nicknamed Grim Reaper to do when a departed witness won't fess up, and she finds herself living with her crazy, arrogant, yet irresistibly sexy boss? Everyone's got secrets, but only the ghosts know whose will be revealed in this hilariously wicked romp in the Paranormal in Manhattan Mystery Series.

Wicked Little Secret is part of the Paranormal in Manhattan Mystery series. If you like fast-paced mysteries full of quirky characters and unexpected twists, you're gonna love *Wicked Little Secret*.

Buy *Wicked Little Secret* and start solving your next mystery today!

Paranormal in Manhattan Mystery Series
Each book in the series is a stand-alone story, but your enjoyment of each story will be increased if you

read them all.
* Book 1-Wicked for Hire
* Book 2-W is for Wicked
* Book 3-Wicked Little Secret
* Book 4-Wicked of the Christmas Past
* Book 5-Sweet Wicked of Mine

Excerpt:

"By the way, are there any rooms off-limits to me?"

"No. Why?" he said, frowning.

"Well, this place reminds me of Christian Grey's penthouse, so I assumed maybe you have something you'd like to hide from me—such as a torture room."

It was supposed to be a joke, but Rick sucked in air. "How did you know that? Actually, I've got seven of them in the upstairs. Each room has uniquely themed décor and equipment for you know what."

"What?" My eyes widened. It was my turn to gasp for air. "Not just one but seven torture rooms?"

"Yup, so I can shift them every day of the week. I'm sure you'll like them." He winked and ran his finger across my lips. "Don't tell anyone, it's my dirty little secret that I have those rooms."

I opened my mouth to say something, but words failed to come, so I nodded like a bobble-head.

"Good girl." Glancing at his splinted and heavily bandaged right leg, he said casually, "The stairs are a bitch to climb up and down on crutches, so I'd appreciate it if you'd bring down the handcuffs and whips, along with a silk blindfold and hogtie. Oh, I've got a can of whipped cream in the fridge. We'll have tons of fun." He winked.

Book 4: Wicked of the Christmas Past:
http://amzn.to/2heVZIQ

Deck the halls with wows of wicked!

FREE on Kindle Unlimited!

A romantic getaway to a posh spa with her devastatingly sexy boss seems like a Christmas miracle to FBI special assistant Amanda Meyer, but when you work for the bureau's Paranormal Cases Division, disaster never takes a holiday.

Bestselling author Carina Christien is dead, her apparent suicide covered up for a year. There's no shortage of suspects, but this is one case that won't be wrapped up neatly. Confessions ring false, intrigue runs high, but even a bevy of disgruntled ghostwriters is no match for the girl they call the Ghost Whisperer. It's mistletoe and murder for Christmas in this fast-paced, quirky, fourth installment of the Paranormal in Manhattan Mystery Series.

PI Assistant Extraordinaire Mysteries:

Book 1: Ghostly Murder: http://amzn.to/2O4aWJ4

A murder in a locked room...

A faceless ghost...

Throw in a cross-dressing detective-savant plus his assistant extraordinaire in this new mystery series!

A high profile murder calls for a high profile detective.

When the famous Sushi Czar is found dead in a room that's locked from the inside, the evidence just doesn't add up. Of course a killer ghost (supernatural killer) is no match for the deductive skills of Michael Archangel. The fabulous cross-dressing former FBI agent can rock a set of sky high stilettos and assemble clues like puzzle pieces, but can he actually prove a ghost committed murder?

Only his assistant knows for sure. Former housewife and London socialite Kelly Kinki (it's Kinki ending with an I not a Y) may someday be the Watson to Archangel's Holmes, but for now, she's following orders, coveting his fashion sense and learning from the master PI that there's something truly fishy about this case.

CHAPTER 1

There's a first time for everything.

I was walking in the forest all by myself. It was a sunny day in late March, but in the shadows of tall trees, it was dark, cold, and creepy. Also, having a group of crows—a.k.a. a *murder* of crows—squawking over my head did nothing to calm my nerves.

Don't get me wrong. I was not an adventurer wannabe or a plant hunter wandering about some exotic forest in the middle of nowhere with a totally unpronounceable name, such as *Tweebuffelsmeteenskootmorsdoodgeskietfontein* in Africa. On the contrary, I was one of those so-called city workers. My job title was the personal assistant to a certain private investigator based in McLean, Virginia.

I was in Arlington, the 'good' suburb of Washington DC. Though there was a metro station in walking distance, this part of the town was very quiet, giving it the feel of a godforsaken land. I wasn't exaggerating. Maybe the fact that a man's dead body was found nearby had something to do with my perception. In addition, considering he was stabbed to death, this neighborhood might not be such a good area. Oh, did I mention there was some wacko serial rapist still running loose in the neighborhood? As a woman with no expertise in martial arts, I had a gazillion reasons to be spooked.

Walking in the forest wasn't something I was doing by choice. Michael Archangel, my eccentric employer with a diva personality, made me do so. My mission was to look for either pantyhose, a ski mask, or big granny panties. Any of those items were supposed to help my employer with his most recent case, but I couldn't figure out why or how. Anyway, I had never dreamed about going treasure-hunting for potentially used undergarments in the urban forest at the age of twenty-nine.

When I was a kid, I wanted to be an alchemist or a doctor. But the reality wasn't rosy enough to realize either of my childhood dreams. First of all, there was no alchemist school. In addition, my test score wasn't good enough for premed programs. So my mom and fifth—or was it sixth?—faux-dad sent me to a finishing school in Switzerland where I mastered the art of eating an orange using a knife and a fork. After that, I became a housewife in London, obtained a bachelor's degree in art, and then I got a divorce. People in Europe, especially rich people in London, still called me 'the bitch who used to be married to that swindler' a.k.a. the man who had committed the largest investment scam in the history of Great Britain.

Here's my point: Education is so overrated.

My name is Kelly Kinki. Yes, it's my real name as written on my birth certificate. No, my surname is not a joke. And no, I'm not into kinky sex. Kinky or otherwise, it had been a while since I had sex.

As I thought about sex, I realized how much I hated walking through the creepy woods. I could think of much better things to do—such as tackling crossword puzzles or building a robot vacuum cleaner from scratch—but sometimes, you had to do what you had to do.

All of the sudden, one of the crows let out an especially menacing squawk as something started chirping and vibrating at the same time, startling me.

"Holy crap!"

A second later, I realized it was coming from my purse and reached for my phone.

"Hello? What can I do for you, Mr. Archangel?" I said to the person on the other end, who happened to be the one responsible for my current situation.

There was no response.

"Hello? Mr. Archangel?"

Still nothing.

From the other end, I could hear muffled voices. I recalled a bunch of retired gentlemen, who resided in the neighborhood, gathering at the crime scene. When I left there, they were busy gossiping. In my mind's eyes, I could almost see and hear them cracking jokes and laughing their *as*—I mean, laughing their *pants* off. A moment later, I finally got a whispered response from Archangel.

"Password."

"What? Password? What are you talking about?" I said, puzzled.

"You need to provide the password of Michael Archangel Investigations."

"Excuse me? I've got your name on my caller ID. And it's my voice. You can recognize me from my voice, can't you?"

"No. You sound different," he said. "Actually, you sound pretty much annoyed."

"Come on, so I'm pretty much annoyed right now, but still, it's me. Besides that, you're the one who's calling my phone, so you should know—" I was tempted to go on with my rant, but I realized it was easier to just tell the password.

"All right! I'll tell the password." Then I stopped short. What was the password? I knitted my eyebrows. It was something about artists. Oh yeah—Matisse, Bonnard, and Rothko—that was it.

"Matisse, Bonnard," I said my part and waited for him to say "Rothko" but—

"Okay, let's get to the point."

"Hey!" I protested. "You're supposed to finish the password before getting to the point. I said 'Matisse, Bonnard' and you're supposed to say 'Rothko.' Without your finishing, the password isn't complete!"

"What are you babbling, Kelly? It's me, Michael Archangel. You should be able to recognize me from my voice. Otherwise, you must be affected with an early-onset of Alzheimer's."

All right, he had a point. The password was pretty much worthless since I knew I was talking to Archangel. His voice was deep, husky, and somewhat seductive, per usual. In addition, I knew no one else as fuc—I mean, *freaking* annoying as him.

"So, what's up, Mr. Archangel? Any progress?"

"Yeah. The cops found the item I was looking for. I knew it was somewhere in the ground. Anyway, you can come back to the tennis court."

"What? So you sent me to this creepy forest fully knowing I wouldn't be the one to find the granny panties?"

"Actually, the discovered item turned out to be a ghost mask."

"That's not the point. You sent me, of all people, to go into this deep, spooky, and potentially dangerous forest for a wild goose chase of a ghost mask you didn't even bother to mention in the first place. On top of it all, I'm talking about these woods located near the site where a twenty-four-year-old female office worker was nearly raped last night for Pete's sake!" I spat.

I knew about her because, this morning, local news was all about this serial rapist in Arlington. In the past month, at least five women had been brutally raped. I was more than concerned about my own safety.

"Good thing you're much older than twenty-four years old," was Archangel's reply.

"Excuse me? That's not the point." I continued. "This rapist has not yet been ID'd, much less arrested. Has it ever come to your mind that the rapist is still hiding in the darkness of these woods, determined to assault another young, innocent, and defenseless woman, such as your assistant? Imagine it. I might become his next prey. Aren't you worried about me?"

Without responding to my bullets of questions, he said, "Come back to the tennis court pronto. If you don't come back before I finish wrapping up the case, I'll leave without you."

And the line went dead.

Words like *manners* and *protocol* must be missing from my employer's dictionary.

Man, I really, *really* hated this job.

Book 2: Immortal Eyes: http://amzn.to/1T4DKC3

Serial murder with a sick ritual...

The most unusual way to use Eggs Benedict...

The mismatched duo's race against time...

Former London socialite Kelly Kinki doesn't always see eye to eye with her sexy-as-hell boss Michael Archangel, but she'll follow the brilliant, cross-dressing detective anywhere to help solve their latest case.

Kelly was happy to lay her rep as the Dragon Lady to rest when she moved across the pond, but to catch an eyeball snatching serial killer she'll have to put her skills at fire breathing to the test once again.

A gruesome autopsy, a visit with her ex, and a shocking encounter with a killer compete for craziest day on the job, but nothing can hold a candle to a glimpse of her boss in the buff.

Can Kelly and Archangel solve the case? The ayes have it. PI's that is.

Chapter 1

There's a first time for everything.

I was at a medical examiner's office in rural Virginia. It was my first visit to this place and, actually, it also happened to be my very first trip to a morgue. I was there to attend the autopsy of a woman who allegedly had fallen victim to a brutal murder. So far, I'd seen more than my share of corpses in the past four months; however, I usually saw them at crime scenes and not morgues.

I didn't know much about the statistics of murders, but I had seen lots of homicide victims since starting this job. In the beginning, I kept track of the body count, but I stopped counting after hitting ten on the third day of my current employment. Later, I learned it was just a temporary thing—one of those crazy, busy times—the "on-season" of killing. Anyway, who knew murders had on-seasons? And I'm not talking about Walmart jobs during the holiday season or the wedding industry in June.

My name is Kelly Kinki. Yes, it's my real name as written on my birth certificate. No, I'm not into kinky sex, and no, I'm not making this surname thing up. I'm twenty-nine years old, half Italian-English American and half Japanese. Currently, I'm divorced with no intention or anticipation of a new romantic relationship, much less marriage.

Been there, done that. No thank you very much.

Right then, my mind was completely centered on my career. And guess what, thinking about myself as a super-cool, classy, and oh-so-savvy sleuth—the assistant extraordinaire, to be precise—totally made me happy. The hard bench chair I sat on was no Cassina, and with the faded grayish-green color scheme, sad taste in décor—or lack thereof—and chilly yet stale air, the morgue's waiting room was depressing at the best of times. But I was optimistic. In fact, I was feeling kind of flamboyant because I really, *really* liked the idea of visiting the morgue in line of my job. First of all, I loved the *CSI* TV series, and the prospect of seeing a live autopsy was totally thrilling. Besides that, it was not like the morgues were open to the public so that anybody could take a sightseeing tour and attend an autopsy, right? Having access to this facility was a real privilege.

In my mind, I was picturing myself as a female version of Dr. John Watson, only less geeky. Maybe by taking a part in the autopsy, I might come up with something that could lead to a breakthrough—just like super-assistants of brilliant detectives in fictions do all the time. Maybe I could even kick some ass like a badass assistant, too. In my opinion, it was often the assistant extraordinaire who should get the credit for disentangling the mystery before his/her boss did.

Something warm and fuzzy started to bubble up in my stomach. It wasn't the aftereffect of a lunch burrito. I had to use a great amount of self-restraint to keep myself from singing, *"For the first time in forever, I'll be watching an autopsy!"* like a certain Princess of Arendelle.

I didn't realize I was smiling until I heard, "Why don't you stop grinning like an idiot?" in a deep, husky voice, which belonged to Michael Archangel, the private investigator I worked for, who was sitting next to me on the same bench.

How I managed to forget his presence, I didn't know. If nothing else, the delicate yet distinct scent of Higher Energy by Dior, his fragrance de jour, should have alerted me to his presence.

No thanks to his voice, I was snapped back to the reality that it was him who had access to the morgue, not me. I hadn't clarified with the morgue, but considering I had no authority or qualification, they wouldn't have granted me permission to attend the autopsy if I went there all by myself. I also realized a *real* badass woman wouldn't imagine singing like a Disney Princess while sitting in the morgue's waiting room. The truth was, I wasn't very sure if I *wanted* to attend the autopsy at all.

I was no Dr. Watson. I had no background in medicine. The closest experience I'd ever had with this particular field was having a pediatrician and an orthopedic surgeon as ex-faux-dads. It was the first time for me to see a cadaver getting cut open. The corpses I had seen often had a hole or two, but I had never seen the human innards peekabooing from inside of the body cavity, saying something like "Yoo-hoo?"

As I anticipated this new experience, a gazillion butterflies went wild in my stomach. Okay, so the earlier flamboyance and faux-hardboiled tone were only parts of my façade to hide my nervousness. And speaking of body contents, I wasn't sure if I'd be able to keep my lunch burrito where it belonged.

Discreetly, I took a deep breath to calm my nerves and regain my composure. "I didn't realize you were watching every step of mine, but thanks for your keen attention anyway. I'm flattered," I said nonchalantly.

"Ha." With a snort, Archangel's candy-apple-colored lips curled into a sarcastic smirk. "Don't get me wrong; it's hard to miss someone sitting by my side babbling silly things with goofy grin pasted on her face, especially when this special someone starts drooling."

I felt around my lips with my fingertips, only to find the area completely drool-free.

"I wasn't drooling. You tricked me!" I narrowed my eyes.

"It's because you're such a good comic relief to poke fun at, Kelly," he had the audacity to admit.

"But look on the bright side. It was just a joke and not a con. Hey, speaking of a con, did I mention I in no compare to the lying, cheating, jilting, swindling, oh-so-disturbing excuse for a human douchebag who happens to be your ex-husband?" With a lighthearted chuckle, he added, "No pun intended."

Biting my lip, I toyed with the idea of kicking him really hard in the shin. This cra...I mean, *nonsense*, of him dissing Warren and my past marriage was just getting old, and it was oh-so-tempting to finally make a point. But I thought better of it. First off, kicking your employer runs a potentially hazardous risk for your job security. Secondly, most of his words were accurate, especially the part about my ex being a con—as in being a convicted conman. I didn't want to reinforce his cocksureness by getting upset. That would only tip him off that yours truly, indeed, had *feelings* for my ex-husband.

So instead of kicking him, I retorted, "I never drool!"

"Hey, Kelly." Flashing the perfect set of pearly whites, Archangel nudged my elbow. "Look what you've done to her." I followed his gaze and spotted the female receptionist. She was practically gaping at us from behind the counter. My eyes met with hers. I tried a polite, social smile that implied I was not her enemy. She averted her gaze.

"See?" He cocked his head. "You've managed to creep her out in five minutes. What a shame. Now I'm labeled as a PI who's stuck with a weird assistant from La-La Land. Come on, I've got a reputation to maintain." As he shook his head, shining locks of his long, auburn hair swayed like dancing waves.

"I see, so you've got a reputation to maintain."

Rephrasing his words, I gave him an up-and-down look. His attire consisted of a skintight, above-the-knee-length dress in vivid magenta and purple fishnet stockings paired with fuck-me-if-you-can high heels. Okay, so the colorful attire flattered his alabaster complexion and the totally gorgeous hair that went midway down his back. Even the heavy makeup wasn't laughable.

Yes, you heard me right. I said he was dressed like a woman. I'm not making any of this up. His outfit de jour was described as skimpy and eye-catching, at best. It was not his Halloween costume on an account that it was early April, not the last day of October. Did I mention that cross-dressing was his "casual/business" attire? I didn't know and didn't want to know what he wore for black-tie events.

I glanced back at the receptionist, who was shaking her head as if trying to clear away the many thoughts running through her mind. I suspected she was taken aback—no, that would be an understatement. I wouldn't be surprised if her brain was caught in a temporary cerebral arrest. Archangel had that effect for many people. Basically, unlike L.A. or Miami, seeing a transvestite in rural Virginia was a very rare occasion, which alone counted as an element of surprise. There was another major element called confusion. Indeed, to the casual eye, his appearance was very confusing. I'm not talking about an esthetically challenged dude playing dress up as a geisha.

He wasn't ugly—lucky him—thanks to inheriting high cheekbones, baby-blue eyes, a well-sculpted nose in a perfect shape that would make Cleopatra cry with envy, and a tall, slender figure from both his mother—Miss California—and grandmother—Miss Greek—he managed to appear almost as strikingly gorgeous as a woman. At least in photos.

Speaking of photos, I supposed perhaps she had seen the pictures of him in the morning paper. Newspapers often carried his photographs. As a Virginia-based PI, he usually consulted with law enforcement, such as the FBI, and worked on tricky, weird, or even the most impossible cases. As a matter of fact, he happened to be a good detective—not just good, but top-notch. He always cracked difficult cases quickly, and as result, newspapers, magazine articles, websites, and sometimes even TV shows reported his accomplishments.

Then again, seeing him in person was a whole different story. Archangel happened to have an even bigger impact in person. He still looked *almost* like a woman. To be precise, he looked more like a supermodel than a woman. I mean, it's not like supermodels look like the rest of us *real* women, right? Those tall, skinny girls are byproducts of women-hating men who dominate the fashion industry and set out to punish us real women by force-feeding us distorted body images, just because we have curves and boobs.

Okay, enough with my little speech. I had mixed feelings about my employer's looks. I know his outfit preference was none of my business, and I believe everyone's entitled to express themselves through fashion. I also appreciated he was the one who caught all the attention, not me. I was the shadow. I enjoyed my invisibility. Then again, it got *a little* awkward when total strangers would stare at us, chattering about 'That totally dazzling supermodel,' and they went on like, 'Who's she? The little one standing next to her? An assistant wannabe? Doesn't she look so mediocre and a little bit heavy?'

And it got *a little* annoying when Archangel caught such chatter and would announce, 'Did you hear that? They think I'm pretty and you're not!'

Did I mention he has a diva personality?

Yeah, it's pretty clear, I ain't no size two. But in my defense, I've got the boobs, uterus, ovaries, and everything a girl needs. Besides that, it's totally rude to judge people based on the physical features for Pete's sake! I might be described as a petite woman, but that doesn't make me *the little one*. I'm the assistant, not a wannabe. Besides that, if you looked carefully, Archangel's jaw was a little bit too strong for a woman and he has an Adam's apple. At 6'3" with lots of toned muscles, what he resembled the most was a Greek Goddess with excessive growth hormone. Or Poseidon in drag.

"Mr. Archangel, why do you think I'm the one who's responsible for spooking her out? Has it ever occurred to you that maybe you're the one who's grabbing her full attention?" I asked.

"Why?" Without answering my question, he arched an eyebrow.

"First of all, she's looking in our direction in general, so both of us are in her sights, and…" I struggled with the words.

"And?" he probed, tapping the backrest of the bench chair with his fingers, which sported nail polish in the same shade of color as the lips.

I was ready to tell him, "And… with all due respect, a giant transvestite is very eye-catching—or rather, an eyesore?" Then it dawned on me that maybe dissing your employer might not be a good move. Call me desperate, but I wasn't made of money and I needed to pay my credit card balance. Unlike Mom, I wasn't a rich-husband-magnet, which meant I really needed to keep my job as a personal assistant to this huge, cross-dressing, brilliant-yet-cynical detective. Maybe I shouldn't have purchased those pricy pillows from Neiman Marcus, but they were so worth it. You want to invest in high-quality pillows to ensure beauty sleep and sweet dreams, especially when you see murdered corpses on a regular basis.

Also, I knew the chances of my scoring other gainful employment anytime soon were practically nonexistent. My resume wasn't something described as highly-decorated. On top of all that, it's not like having lost my last employer in a tragic murder—which wasn't my fault but made me look like a jinx—*and* being an ex-wife of a notorious swindler would catch a potential employer's attention in a good way, would it?

Yes, I was desperate. So much for an independent woman ready to kick ass.

"Kelly? Tell me why you think I'm the one who's creeping her out." Crossing his long legs, Archangel pressed on.

"Well…" With all due respect, I furrowed my eyebrows like a confused third-grader struggling to grasp the concept of division. "What was I thinking? Isn't it odd that I can't recollect whatever was in my head?"

"Ha. You need to get a head CT to see if you've got a brain at all." Archangel gave a throaty, husky, oh-so-manly laugh. Did I mention his voice was often a dead giveaway for his otherwise confusing gender? When I first met him, I thought he must be gay, but I wasn't so sure any more. I knew his sexual orientation was none of my business, and I respected people with every sexuality, but for a guy who opted to wear women's clothes, Archangel was pretty much lacking delicacy.

Turning my face away from him, I stuck out my tongue. Very mature, I knew. So far, my job duties were one part secretary, one part chauffeur, and one part personal chef. Not to mention being a part-time comic, or rather, laughing stock. Unlike brilliant detectives in literature, Archangel didn't need much assisting when it came to investigation and solving cases. Just like fictional detectives, he was crazy and tended to torment his precious little assistant, having a chuckle at my expense.

I was an assistant extraordinaire who outshone the detective only in my fantasy, and in reality, I was merely a newbie assistant and a butt of jokes to this huge, cross-dressing detective.

It really sucked when the gap between your fancy daydream and the hard, cold, stone-hearted reality was so huge.

Book 3: Deadly Vision: http://amzn.to/1og0Pp9

A sweet n' cold murder…

A newbie, pathetic agent…

And a hot mess…

PI Assistant extraordinaire Kelly Kinki is back, and she's stuck between a hunk and a hard case.

A popular college student has been murdered after visiting a local ice cream shop. The suspect list is short and sweet, but with a fledgling FBI agent tagging along on their investigation, Kelly and her drop dead gorgeous boss Michael Archangel have an extra scoop of trouble.

Trading his dress for a suit and hitting DC's top ten list of eligible bachelors may be business as usual for Archangel, but with a hopeless newbie screwing up the case and Kelly revving up his libido, solving this seemingly ordinary murder might not be cake for America's answer to Sherlock Holmes.

CHAPTER 1

There's a first time for everything.

I was engaged in a tight lip-lock with Michael Archangel, a Virginia-based private investigator and my employer.

There should have been a sequence of events that led to the incident, but I couldn't recall anything at all. And for full disclosure, I was way too preoccupied with the current action to care about how I ended up in a hot kiss with him.

Just like in cartoons, the angel part of me was

sitting on my right shoulder, screaming things like "Hello! What's happened to your professionalism? Don't you have anything like work ethics?" And the devil part of me was hooting, jumping, and cheering me from on my other shoulder. "Go, Kelly, go! Think about it, you're not getting any younger!" She was a really naughty devil.

As a professional woman with work ethics and dignity, I didn't listen to the devil and started listening to the angel, and…no, that's a lie. I didn't listen to the angel. Call me an unethical slut, but I was falling for the devil's words.

For a brief moment, our lips parted. I opened my eyes. His baby blues were staring at me so intensely, they seemed a shade or two darker than usual.

He cupped my face in his hands.

"Are you ready?" he whispered. His voice sounded oh-so-sweet on my ears. Then he brushed away my hair and planted a light peck on my forehead.

I mumbled something that meant nothing and everything. Then I realized he was shirtless and I was only one slutty Agent Provocateur bra and a thong away from…*gulp!* the bedroom.

Breathing hard and admiring his Greek god-like physique, I struggled with his belt buckle, which didn't unbuckle easily. I shivered as Archangel unhooked my bra with just a snap of his fingers.

I closed my eyes. He was reaching south, and then…

* * *

Also, there's a bundle of 3 books available… Confessions of the Assistant Extraordinaire: amzn.to/1R3GaO6

Made in the USA
Middletown, DE
17 September 2017